PRAISE FOR *NAKED*

"Raine Miller delivers a seductive and masterful chase of erotic exchanges between her beautifully flawed characters."

—DEMONLOVER'S BOOKS & MORE

"*Naked* is fast-paced, sexy and a clever piece of writing."

—TOTALLY BOOKED

"How the story plays out, the way characters are portrayed and the skill of the author's writing, is what differentiates books and sets them apart. This one shoots straight to the top!!"

—SWEPT AWAY BY ROMANCE

"Raine Miller does an amazing job of building the sexual chemistry in the lead up to Ethan and Brynne's first sexual encounter—it's sizzling hot and sure doesn't disappoint!!"

—SINFULLY SEXY

"5 STARS for *Naked*! Fall in love with Ethan and thank me later when you agree *Naked* is fantastic! One final statement . . . Christian who?"

—AUTHOR DM MCDANIEL

"*Naked* will lure you in, the characters will intrigue you and the story will keep you wanting more."

—TALK SUPE

"The title of this book is so aptly named as the characters are stripped 'Naked' to their bare feelings and what they do to one another."

—FLIRTY AND DIRTY BOOK BLOG

"Tastefully erotic."

—KELLY OAKES

"I was hooked within the first few lines of this book and could not put it down."

—AUTHOR RHONDA PLUMHOFF

ALSO BY RAINE MILLER

All In: The Blackstone Affair, Book 2

Naked

THE BLACKSTONE AFFAIR

BOOK 1

RAINE MILLER

ATRIA PAPERBACK

New York • London • Toronto • Sydney • New Delhi

ATRIA PAPERBACK
A Division of Simon & Schuster, Inc.
1230 Avenue of the Americas
New York, NY 10020

First Atria Paperback edition May 2013

ATRIA PAPERBACK and colophon are trademarks of Simon & Schuster, Inc.

For information about special discounts for bulk purchases, please contact Simon & Schuster Special Sales at 1-866-506-1949 or business@simonandschuster.com.

The Simon & Schuster Speakers Bureau can bring authors to your live event. For more information or to book an event contact the Simon & Schuster Speakers Bureau at 1-866-248-3049 or visit our website at www.simonspeakers.com.

10 9 8 7 6 5 4 3

Library of Congress Cataloging-in-Publication Data

Miller, Raine
Naked : the Blackstone Affair, book 1 / Raine Miller. — First Atria Books trade paperback edition.
     p. cm. — (Blackstone Affair ; 2)
  1. Romantic suspense fiction. I. Title.
  PS3613.I547N35 2013
  813'.6—dc23   2012049352

ISBN 978-1-4767-3524-5
ISBN 978-1-4767-3525-2 (ebook)

Franziska

My dear friend, this is for you . . .

Truth! stark naked truth, is the word.

—JOHN CLELAND, 1749

Acknowledgments

The idea for *Naked* is something I feel I should share with my readers. You never know what will spark initiative for a story, and for me, the seed of inspiration for the Blackstone Affair was a total surprise. While looking for stock images one afternoon to be used as a potential book cover for another story, I stumbled upon the photo of a nude woman in a tasteful pose—the image on the cover of this book right now. I was so taken with it I had to sit down and write. Within an hour I had the first chapter of Brynne, the model, meeting Ethan, the man who'd just bought a portrait of her naked self. The story had me in its grip by this point, and I was totally lost in it. My other projects had to be set aside so I could devote my time to writing this new series. And I consider it a blessing, because finding the photograph that day pushed me to create this exciting world and these very special characters of the Blackstone Affair. I love being able to invent the people in my books. Thank you to Kim Killion of Hot Damn Designs for creating such a rockin' cover to accompany this story. To Kathe for finding the font. She was relentless.

Now, with that being said, I want to thank a few people for the kind words, help, support, questions, advice, enthusiasm, pats on the back, hand-holding, drive-by love bombs, and just good old-fashioned friendship, for without it, I would not have this book to share, nor would being a writer be something that I love as much as I do. So, to Franzi, Bels, Stacie, Angel, Lisa, Kristy, TJ, Rebecca, Donna, Ai-vy, Mandy, Melina, Rhonda, Lacey, Sherie, Sarah, Carolyn, Kristin, Michelle, Colleen and my three guys: *Muah*

Love you much, respect you more.

Raine

Naked

THE BLACKSTONE AFFAIR

BOOK 1

Prologue

May 2012
London

I don't know shit about American politics. I don't need to know. I'm a British citizen and Parliament is confusing enough. Politics don't interest me much. But I am forced to work around the by-products of political affairs all the time. I deal in security, both private and for the British government. I'm good at my job. I take it very seriously. In my business you have to be good, because when you're not good people die.

United States congressman goes down in a plane crash. Newsworthy, of course. But when said congressman was the probable vice presidential nominee for the challenging party and the election is mere months away, then it makes world news in a viral heartbeat. Especially when people who want the power will do just about anything to ensure the incumbent never stands a second term. Scrambling for a replacement, the GOP understandably needed to fill the empty slot on their ticket. And this is how I came to discover her.

I received the email from her father first. A voice from my past extending a friendly greeting and an acknowledgment of where we'd both ended up. Fair enough. My past had been a colorful one, including both the good and the bad, and he'd come into my life during one of the good parts.

A phone call came next, when he told me he had a daughter living in London. He was concerned about her safety and gave some tentative details explaining why. I was polite and felt quite sure I didn't need to involve myself. My job had me overextended as it was. Organizing VIP security for London 2012 at the XXX Olympiad pretty much consumed all my time, and I had nothing to spare for the daughter of an acquaintance I'd met at a poker tournament more than six years gone.

I told him no. As a personal favor, I was even prepared to give him a referral to another private security firm when he played his hand. Poker players know when to play their hands.

He sent me her picture in a second email.

That picture changed everything. I was not the same after I saw it, and I couldn't go back to the man I'd been before seeing it either. Not after we met that night on the street. My whole world altered because of a photograph. A photograph of my beautiful American girl.

Chapter 1

My mother can't see this right now, and that's a really good thing. She would freak. I'd made it to Benny's show tonight because I told him I'd be here and I know how important it is for him. It's important for me too. I only want the best for my friend, just like he does for me. In the past three years Benny has been right there to console me, drink with me, commiserate with me, and even to help me pay my rent upon occasion by giving me work. Well, that and the fact he shot the photograph I'm staring at right now. And it's a picture of my nude body.

Posing as a nude model isn't something I dreamed

of doing for my life's work or anything, but it is a way to make some extra money in between student loans. And lately I'd been getting offers from other photographers. Benny said to be prepared for more interest too, because of this show tonight. *People will inquire about the model. It's a given, Brynne.* That's my Benny, always the optimist.

I sipped my champagne and studied the really huge image hanging on the gallery wall. My portrait had been enlarged and printed on canvas for this show. The effect was a bit startling but even so, it was apparent that Benny had talent. For a child of Somali refugees who started with less than nothing in the UK, he knew how to con- figure a picture. He'd posed me on my back with my head turned to the side, my arm over my breasts and my fin- gers flared between my legs. He'd wanted my hair splayed out, my legs straight up, and my puss covered. I'd worn a string thong for the shot, but you couldn't see it. Nothing showed that would classify my image as porn. The proper term is *artistic nude photography,* anyway. My stuff was shot tastefully or I didn't do it. Well, I certainly hoped my pictures didn't get onto any porn sites, but who could know for sure these days. I didn't do porn. I hardly did sex.

"There's my girl!" Benny's big arms wrapped around my shoulders and he rested his chin on top of my head. "It's smashing isn't it? And you have the most beautiful feet of any woman on the planet."

"Everything you do looks good, Ben, even my feet." I

turned around and faced him. "So, you sell anything yet? Let me rephrase. How *many* have you sold?"

"Three so far, and I think this one's going very soon." Ben winked. "Don't be obvious, but see the tall bloke in the gray suit, black hair, speaking with Carole Andersen? He's inquired. Seems he's quite taken by your gorgeous naked self. Probably going to go for a good palm session soon as he can get the canvas all to himself. How's that make you feel, Brynne, luv? Some rich toff pulling his pud to the sight of your unearthly beauty."

"Shut up." I rolled my eyes at him. "That's just nasty. Don't tell me things like that or I'll have to stop taking jobs." I tilted my head and shook it. "It's a damn good thing I love you, Benny Clarkson." Ben could say the crassest thing and manage to make it come out proper and refined. Must be his British accent. Hell, even Ozzy Osbourne sounded proper at times thanks to that accent.

"It's true, though," Ben said, placing a kiss on my cheek, "and you know it. That chap hasn't stopped eyeballing you since you glided in here. And he's not gay."

I gaped at Benny. "Good to know. Thank you, Ben, for the update. And I don't glide!"

He grinned at me in that wicked, boyish way of his. "Believe me, if he was I would've offered to blow him in the back room by now. He's off-the-charts hot."

"You're going to hell, you know that, don't you?" I looked over casually and checked out the buyer. Benny was right about him; the guy oozed hotness from the leather soles of his Ferragamos to the tips of his wavy dark hair. About six foot three, muscular, confident, rich. I couldn't tell about his eyes because he was talking to the owner of the gallery. About my picture maybe? Hard to say, but didn't matter anyway. Even if he did buy it, I'd never see him again.

"I'm right, huh?" Ben saw me looking and nudged me in the ribs.

"About the jerking off? No possible way, Benny!" I shook my head slowly. "He's far too beautiful to have to resort to his hand for an orgasm."

And then that beautiful man turned and looked at me. His eyes burned across the room almost as if he'd heard what I'd just said to Benny. But that was impossible. Wasn't it? He kept staring and I finally had to look down. There was no way I could compete with that level of intensity, or whatever the hell was coming at me from where he stood. The urge to flee kicked in immediately. Safety first.

I gulped another swig from my champagne and drained it. "I need to go now. And the show is brilliant." I hugged my friend. "And you will be famous the world over," I told him, grinning. "In about fifty more years!"

Benny laughed behind me as I headed for the door. "Call me, my lovely!"

I waved a hand without turning and stepped out. The

street was busy for London on a weeknight. The upcoming Olympic Games had turned the city into an absolute cluster of humanity. It could be years before I got a cab. Should I risk the walk to the closest Underground station? I glanced down at my heels, which looked great paired with my dress but were seriously lacking in the walking-comfort department. And even if I took the Tube, I'd still have to hoof it another couple blocks to my flat in the dark. Mom would say not to, of course. But then again, Mom wasn't here in London. Mom was home in San Francisco, where I didn't want to be. *Screw this.* I started walking.

"It's a very bad idea, Brynne. Don't risk it. Let me give you a ride."

I froze on the street. I knew who spoke to me without ever having heard his voice before. I turned slowly to face the same eyes that had burned me back at the gallery. "I don't know you at all," I told him.

He smiled, his lip turning up more on one side than the other of his goateed mouth. He pointed to his car at the curb, a sleek black Range Rover HSE. The kind that only Brits with money can ever afford. Not that he didn't reek of money before, but he was way out of my league.

I swallowed hard in my throat. Those eyes of his were blue, very clear and deep. "Yet you call me by name and—and expect me to get in a car with you? Are you crazy?"

He walked toward me and extended his hand. "Ethan Blackstone."

I stared at his hand, so finely elegant with the white cuff framing the gray sleeve of his designer jacket. "How do you even know my name?"

"I just bought a work entitled *Brynne's Repose* from the Andersen Gallery for a nice sum not fifteen minutes ago. And I'm fairly sure I'm not mentally impaired. Sounds more PC than *crazy,* don't you think?" He kept his hand out.

I met his hand and he took mine. Oh, did he ever. Or maybe I'd lost my mind shaking hands with the stranger who'd just purchased a huge canvas of my naked body. Ethan possessed a firm grip. And hot too. Had I imagined he pulled me a little closer toward him? Or maybe I was the crazy one, because my feet hadn't moved an inch. Those blue eyes were nearer to me than they were a moment ago, though, and I could smell his cologne. Something so gawd-awfully delicious that it was sinful to smell that good and be human.

"Brynne Bennett," I said.

He let go of my hand. "And now we know each other," he said, pointing first at me and then to himself, "Brynne, Ethan." He motioned with his head toward his Rover. "Now will you let me take you home?"

I swallowed again. "Why do you care so much?"

"Because I don't want anything to happen to you? Because those heels look lovely at the end of your legs but will be hell to walk in? Because it's dangerous for a woman alone at night in the city?" His eyes flicked over me. "Especially one that looks like you." That mouth of his turned up just slightly on the one side again. "So many reasons, Miss Bennett."

"What if you're not safe?" He raised an eyebrow at me. "I still don't know you or anything about you, or if Ethan Blackstone is your real name." *Did he just give me a look?*

"You have a point in that. And it's one I can rectify easily." He reached into his jacket pocket and pulled out a driver's license with the name Ethan James Blackstone clearly printed on it. He handed me a business card with the same name and *Blackstone Security International, Ltd.* engraved on the cream cardstock. "You may keep that." He grinned again. "I'm very busy at my job, Miss Bennett. I have absolutely no time for a hobby as a serial killer, I promise you."

I laughed. "Good one, Mr. Blackstone." I put his card in my purse. "All right. You can give me a ride." His brow shot up again, and I got the sideways grin again too.

I winced inwardly at the double entendre for *ride* and tried to focus on how uncomfortable my shoes really would be for walking to the Tube station, and that it was a good idea to let him drive me.

He pressed his hand to the bottom of my back and led me to the curb. "In you go." Ethan got me settled and then walked around to the street side and slid behind the wheel, smooth as a panther. He looked at me and tilted his head. "And where does Miss Bennett live?"

"Nelson Square in Southwark."

He frowned but then turned his face away and pulled out into traffic. "You are American."

What, he didn't like Americans? "I am here on scholarship at the University of London. Graduate program," I tacked on, wondering why I felt the need to tell him anything at all about myself.

"And the modeling?"

The second he asked the question the sexual tension thickened. I paused before answering. I knew exactly what he was doing—imagining me in my picture. Naked. And as weird as it felt, I opened my mouth and told him. "Um, I—I posed for my friend, the photographer, Benny Clarkson. He asked me, and it helps pay the bills, you know?"

"Not really, but I love the portrait of you, Miss Bennett." He kept his eyes on the road.

I felt myself stiffen at his comment. Who in the hell was he to judge what I do to support myself?

"Well, my own personal international corporation never came through like yours did, Mr. Blackstone. I resorted to modeling. I like sleeping in a bed as opposed to a park bench. And heat. The winters here suck!" The snark in my voice rang out pretty clear even to my ears.

"In my experience I've found many things here that *suck*." He turned and gave me an expert blue-eyed stare.

How he said "suck" got my blood tingling in a way that left no doubts about my skills in fantasy being sound. I might not get a ton of practical experience between the sheets, but my fantasies don't suffer one iota from lack of use.

"Well we agree on something then." I brought my fingers to my forehead and rubbed. The image of Ethan's cock and the word "suck" in the same little space in my brain was a little much at the moment.

"Headache?"

"Yeah. How did you know?"

We slowed for a stoplight and he looked over at me, his eyes traveling from my lap back up to my face in a slow, measured pace. "Merely a guess. No dinner, just the champagne you gulped back at the gallery, and now it's late and your body is putting up a protest." He lifted his eyebrow yet again. "How'd I do?"

I swallowed hard, desperately wishing for water. *Bingo, Mr. Blackstone. You read me like a cheap comic book. Whoever you are, you're good.*

"I just need two aspirin and some water and I'll be fine."

He shook his head at me. "When did you last eat some food, Brynne?"

"So we're back to first names again?"

He gave me a tolerant look but I could tell he was pissed.

"I had a late breakfast, okay? I'll make something when I get home." I looked out the window. The light must have changed, because we started moving again. The only sounds were of his body shifting as he turned the corner. And it was way too sexy of a sound to keep my eyes averted for long. I chanced a peek. In profile, Ethan had a rather prominent nose, but on him it didn't matter; he was still beautiful.

Ignoring me now, acting as if I wasn't sitting two feet from him, he efficiently drove us. Ethan seemed to know his way around London, because he didn't ask me for directions once. I could still smell him, though, and the scent did things to my head. I really needed to get out of the car.

He made a rude noise and pulled into a retail center. "Stay here; I'll be just a minute." His voice sounded a little edgy. A lot more than a little, actually. Everything was edgy with him. And commanding. Like he told you what to do and you didn't dare argue.

The warmth of the car and the coziness of the leather seat felt nice underneath the thin skirt I'd worn tonight. Ethan was right about one thing, I would have died on my walk to the Tube. Here I sat in the car of a virtual stranger, who'd seen me naked, had bullied me into taking a ride, and was now coming out of the convenience store with a bag in his hand and a grim look on his face. This whole situation was weirder than weird.

"What did you need to get in the store—"

He shoved a bottle of water into my hand and opened a single packet of Nurofen, the equivalent of Advil in

Britain. I took both without a word, not caring that he watched me gulp down the pills. The water was gone in under a minute. He set a protein bar on my knee.

"Now eat it." His voice had that don't-fuck-with-me tone again. "Please," he added.

I sighed and opened the white chocolate PowerBar. The crinkle of the wrapper filled the silence in the car as we sat there. I took a bite and chewed slowly. It tasted divine. I had needed what he'd brought me. Desperately.

"Thank you," I whispered, feeling suddenly emotional, the urge to cry bubbling up fiercely. I held it down as best I could. I kept my head down too.

"My pleasure," he said softly. "Everyone needs the basics, Brynne. Food, water . . . a bed."

A bed. The sexual tension was back, or maybe it never left. Ethan seemed blessed with the talent to make the most innocent word sound like hot, sweaty, mind-blowing sex you remembered for a long, long time. He sat beside me and didn't back the car out until I'd finished the last of the protein bar.

"What's your actual street address?" he asked.

"41 Franklin Crossing."

Ethan took us out of the parking lot and headed back onto the street, bringing me closer to my flat with every revolution of the tires. I leaned into the soft leather and closed my eyes. My phone vibrated in my purse. I fished it out and saw there'd been a text from Benny: **u home ok?**

I shot back a quick **yup** and closed my eyes again. I could feel my headache begin to slip away. I felt more relaxed than I'd been in hours. Exhaustion won out, I suppose, because I would have never allowed myself the indulgence of falling asleep in Ethan Blackstone's car if I could possibly have helped it.

Chapter 2

Someone smelled very good as they touched me. I could smell the spice and feel the weight of a hand on my shoulder. But the fear rose up anyway. The blast of terror that brought me screaming into consciousness arrived right on schedule. I knew what it was, but still the panic ruled me. I should know. The feeling had been with me for years now.

"Brynne, wake up."

That voice. Who was it? I opened my eyes and faced into the blue intensity of Ethan Blackstone not more than six inches away. I pushed back into the seat to make more distance between me and that gorgeous face. I remembered now. He bought my picture tonight. And took me home.

"Shit! I'm sorry I—I fell asleep?" I fiddled for the door handle, but I didn't know this car. I scrambled blindly to get out—to get away.

Ethan's hand shot over and covered mine, stilling it with a firm touch. "Easy. You're safe, everything's fine. You just drifted off is all."

"Okay . . . sorry." I panted some deep breaths, looked out the window, and then back to him still watching my every move.

"Why do you keep apologizing?"

"I don't know," I whispered. I did know, but couldn't think about it at the moment.

"Are you okay?" He smiled slowly with a tilt of his head. I swear he liked the fact that he rattled me. I wasn't sure if I didn't. I so needed to get away from this situation right now, before I agreed to all manner of things. Something along the lines of: *Take off your clothes and stretch out in the big backseat of my Range Rover, Brynne.* This man had a way with control that severely unnerved me.

"Thank you for the ride. And the water. And the other stu—"

"You take care of yourself, Brynne Bennett." He pressed a button and the lock clicked. "You have your key ready? I'll wait until you're inside. What floor is it?"

I dug my key out of my purse and replaced it with my phone, which was still on my lap. "I live in the top studio loft, fifth floor."

"Roommate?"

"Well, yes, but she's probably not in." Again, wondering what loosed my tongue in sharing personal information with a virtual stranger.

"I'll look for the light to come on then." Ethan's face was unreadable. I had no idea what he was thinking.

I pushed the door open and got out. "Good night, Ethan Blackstone." I left his car at the curb and headed up the steps of my building, feeling the stare of his eyes as I walked. Sticking the key in the door, I looked back over my shoulder at the Rover. The windows were so dark I couldn't see inside, but he was in there waiting for me to get in my building so he could leave.

I opened the foyer door to five flights of stairs ahead of me. I slipped off the heels and did it barefoot. The second I entered my flat I hit the lights and locked up. I literally collapsed against the wooden door for support. My heels dumped on the floor in a clatter, and I exhaled a huge sigh. *What the hell just happened?*

It took a minute to heave myself away from the damn door and head over to the window. I pulled back the drapes with a finger to find his car gone. Ethan Black-stone was gone.

A five-mile run was just the ticket to help clear my head of the fog from last night's—Alice in Wonderland down a friggin' rabbit hole—trip. I seriously felt like I'd done the whole "Eat Me" and "Drink Me" thing too. Jesus, had the champagne been drugged? I'd acted like it. Allowing an unknown man to drive me in his car, drop me at my home and take over control of my food? Well it was stupid, and I told myself to forget about it and him. Life was complicated enough without borrowing trouble.

That's what Aunt Marie always said. Picturing her reaction to my modeling made me smile. I knew for a fact that my great-aunt was less concerned about the nude pictures than my own mother was. Aunt Marie was no prude. I set my iPod to shuffle and took off.

Pretty soon the awkward encounter from last night had been pounded onto the London pavement of Waterloo Bridge. It felt good to push myself physically and just run. Must be all the endorphins. Cursing inwardly for another sex reference, I wondered if that was my problem, and the reason I allowed Ethan so much leeway last night. Maybe I needed an orgasm. *You're so screwed.* Yeah, and I could just imagine the literal and figurative versions of that statement.

I forged ahead and crossed over onto the Thames path that followed the great river. My iPod helped too. Music had a way of resetting the brain. With Eminem and Rihanna battling out lying for the sake of love in my ears, I kept a steady pace and admired the architecture I passed on my route. The history in as ancient a city as London was vast, yet it contrasted with the bustling, modern world player in a perfect balance. Duality. I loved living here.

Modeling wasn't my only job. All students enrolled in the graduate program for art conservancy at the University of London were required to do practicum duties at the Rothvale Gallery in Winchester House. The Duke of Winchester's seventeenth-century mansion had housed U of L's Department of Art for about fifty years, and in my opinion, a more beautiful location to study certainly did not exist anywhere else.

Heading in through the employee entrance, I flashed my badge for security, then again for the conservation studios.

"Miss Brynne, good day to you." Rory. So proper and formal. The back room guard greeted me the exact same way every time I came in. I kept hoping that one time he would say something different. *Shag any millionaire control freaks last night, Miss Brynne?*

"Hey, Rory." I gave him my best smile as he let me through.

I stayed focused and sharp during my work. The painting was a stunner, one of Mallerton's early works, entitled simply *Lady Percival*. An absolutely compelling woman with nearly black hair, a blue dress to match her eyes, a book in her hand and the most magnificent figure a female could ever hope to have took up most of the canvas. She wasn't so much a beauty as expressive. I very much wished I knew her story. The painting had suffered some heat damage during a fire in the sixties and had never been touched since. Lady Percival needed a dose of tender loving care, and I would be the lucky one to give it to her.

I was just about to go for a break when my phone went off. *Unknown caller?* It struck me odd. I didn't give my number out, and the Lorenzo Agency who represented my modeling had strict disclosure rules.

"Hello?"

"Brynne Bennett." The sexy cadence of a British voice washed over me.

It was him. Ethan Blackstone. How, I have no earthly idea. Or why for that matter, but it was him, sexy accent live and well on the other end of my phone. I would know that commanding voice anywhere.

"How did you get this number?"

"You gave it to me last night." His voice burned into my ear and I knew he was lying.

"No," I said slowly, trying to put the brakes on my escalating heartbeat, "I did not give you my number last night." Why was he calling?

"I *may* have borrowed your phone by accident while you were dozing . . . and called my mobile with it. You distracted me by being dehydrated and starved." I heard muffled voices in the background, like he could be in an office. "It's very easy to pick up the wrong mobile phone when they all look alike."

"So you went into my phone and dialed yours so you could get my number off the history of calls received. That's kinda creepy, Mr. Blackstone." I was starting to get rather pissed at Mr. Tall, Dark and Handsome with the Gorgeous Blue Eyes for his utter lack of personal boundaries.

"Please call me Ethan, Brynne. I want you to call me Ethan."

"And I want you to respect my privacy, *Ethan*."

"Do you, Brynne? I think you're really grateful for the ride home last night." He said in a softer voice, "And you seemed to like your *dinner* too." He paused for a moment. "You thanked me." More silence. "In your condition you would've never made it home safely."

Seriously? His words returned me straight back to the overwhelming emotion I'd felt last night when he'd brought me the water and the Nurofen. And as much as I hated to admit it, he was right.

"Okay . . . look, Ethan, I owe you for the ride last night. It was a good call on your part and I do thank you for the help, but—"

"Then have dinner with me. A proper dinner, preferably not something enclosed in plastic or foil, and definitely not in my car."

"Oh, no. Sorry, but I don't think that's a good ide—"

"You just said, 'Ethan, I owe you for the ride,' and that's what I want—for you to have dinner with me. Tonight."

My heart pounded harder. *I can't do this.* He affected me so strangely. I knew myself well enough to realize that Ethan Blackstone was dangerous territory for a girl like me—Great White Shark is hungry for lone swimmer in cove territory.

"I have plans tonight," I blurted into my phone. A total lie.

"Then tomorrow night."

"I—I can't then. I'll be working late afternoon and photo shoots always exhaust me—"

"Perfect. I'll pick you up from your shoot, feed you, and take you home for an early night."

"You keep interrupting me every time I speak! I can't think straight when you start barking orders, Ethan. Are you like this with everyone, or am I just special?" I did not like how the conversation turned so fast in his favor. It was maddening. And whatever he meant in the way of an early night left me imagining all kinds of forbidden.

"Yes . . . and yes, Brynne, you are." I could feel the sex dripping off his voice through my phone, and it scared the shit out of me. And I am a stupid idiot for wording the question like that. *Way to go, Brynne, Ethan says you're special.*

"I have to get back to work now." My voice sounded thready. I knew it did. He just disarmed me so damn easily. I tried again. "Thanks for the offer, Ethan, but I can't—"

"Say no to me," he interrupted, "and that's why I'll pick you up from the shoot tomorrow for dinner. You admitted that you owe me a favor, and I am calling it in. It's what I want, Brynne."

Fucker did it again! I sighed into the phone loudly and let that sit in silence for a moment. I was not going to give in to him so easily.

"Still there, Brynne?"

"So you want me to talk now? You sure change your mind quickly. Every time I speak you interrupt me. Didn't your mother teach you any manners, Ethan?"

"She couldn't. My mother died when I was four."

Fuck. "Ahhh, well that explains it then. I'm very sorry—look, Ethan, I really have to get back to my work. You take care." I took the chicken way out and ended the call.

I set my cheek on the worktable and just rested for a minute, or five. Ethan wore me out. I don't know how he managed it, but he did. Eventually I got up from my chair and headed for the break room. I got the biggest mug I could find, filled it with a shitload of half-and-half and sugar, and a moderate amount of coffee. Maybe a caffeine and carb buzz would help me, or put me into a coma.

Looking over at my workspace I saw the captivating Lady Percival prepped and waiting for me, elegant and calm as she had been for more than a century. Coffee in hand, I returned to her and attended to cleaning the grime from the book she so lovingly held to her breast.

Chapter 3

Benny's beautiful brown skin looked marvelous against the pale yellow shirt draped onto his muscled frame. Confidence poured out of Benny in every aspect of his life. Totally optimistic. I wish I could be more like him. I was giving it my best shot, but let's just say my best shot at it sucked.

"So this Ethan bloke is trying to get all up in you, huh? I saw how he watched you, Brynne. He never *stopped* looking," Ben muttered, "not that I blame him."

Benny's always been sweet like this. My go-to guy when I need a shoulder. He's nosy, though. I'd tried all night to keep the conversation focused on his photography and gallery show, but he kept steering the talk back to Ethan.

"Yeah, well he has a way of getting the upper hand, and I don't like it, Ben." I dipped my French fry—that I refuse to call a chip—into some ranch dressing and popped it in my mouth. "And thanks for making an honest woman of me tonight." I ate another fry. "I told Ethan I had plans, which was a total lie until you called."

Ben pointed a fry at me and smirked. "So that's why you nearly jumped me through my mobile."

I took a swig of my Sheppy's cider, no longer hungry for the burger and fries. "Thanks for the invite, my friend." Even to my ears I sounded like a bore.

"Well, why don't you go out with him? He's hot. He wants you badly. He can certainly afford to show you a good time." Benny picked up my hand and pressed his soft lips to my skin. "You need to have a little fun, luv. Or a good shag. Everybody needs to get some once in a while. How long's it been?"

I snatched my hand from him and took another swig of Sheppy's. "I am *not* talking about the last time I got laid, Ben. Boundaries much?"

He gave me a patient look. "You definitely need an orgasm, darling."

I ignored his comment. "He's just so—well, I—he's— the man is so dang intense. His words, the stuff he does, the raised brow, those blue eyes—" I pointed my finger at my head like a gun and pulled the trigger. "I can't think when he starts in with the commands." I noticed Ben had pushed his plate away too. "You're ready to go, aren't you?"

"Yeah. Let's get your sexually frustrated vagina home. Maybe you can have a date with your vibrator and that will help."

I kicked Benny in the foot under the table.

During the cab ride to my flat I thought about the previous night in Ethan's car. I obviously felt comfortable enough to fall asleep. That had been a total shocker. I *never* did stuff like that. Ever. With my history, letting my guard down with strangers was not on the menu, especially the sleeping thing. So why had I done so with Ethan? Was it his gorgeous looks? I'd only really seen his face, but I could tell he was built underneath the silk suit. The man had the whole package working for him. Why me, when he could certainly have anyone he wanted?

"So you're booked for a studio shoot tomorrow at Lorenzo?"

"Yeah." I hugged Ben. "Thanks for the referral, honey, and the dinner. You are the best." I kissed him on the cheek. "*Vaya con Dios,* you sexy man."

"Love it when you speak Spanish to me, darling!" Benny motioned with his hands toward his chest. "Keep it coming! I want to impress Ricardo next time he's in town."

I left Ben in the cab with a smile on his face, blowing a kiss. I headed up to my little flat that I love and adore, was in my shower in under five minutes, and in my pajamas another ten after that. I'd just put my toothbrush in the holder when my phone went off. I looked at the display. *Crap.* Ethan.

I hit accept and gathered the courage to speak. "Ethan..."

"I like when you say my name, so I suppose I'll forgive you for hanging up on me today." His slow, elegant Brit voice settled over me, heightening my awareness of his maleness and the promise of sex instantly.

"Sorry about that." I waited for him to say something else, but he didn't. I still hadn't agreed to go out with him, though, and we both knew it.

Finally he asked, "So how were your plans tonight?" I could just picture that mouth of his in a firm line of annoyance.

"They were fine—good. I just got in, actually . . . from dinner."

"And what did you order at your dinner, Brynne?"

"Why must you know, Ethan?"

"So I can learn what pleases you." And just like that he did it again! Taking my defensiveness away with a few small words and dripping of sexual innuendo as always. And making me feel like a cold bitch.

"I had a garden burger, fries, and a Sheppy's cider." I felt myself relax a little and softened my tone.

"Vegetarian?"

"Not at all. I love meat—I mean—I eat ... meat ... all the time." *Dear Lord.* The brief feeling of relaxation vanished instantly and I was back to tripping over my words like a teenager.

Ethan laughed into the phone. "So a good selection of meats and Sheppy's on the menu will do it for you?"

"Hey, I never said I would go out with you." I closed my eyes.

"But you will." His voice did something to me. Even through the phone, without sense of sight, he compelled me to want to agree just to see him again. To look at him again. To smell him again.

I groaned into the phone. "You are killing me here, Ethan."

"No," he chuckled softly, "we've already established that I'm not a serial killer, remember?"

"So you claim, Mr. Blackstone, but know that if you *do* kill me, you'll be number one on the suspect list."

He laughed at that and the sound of him made me smile. "So you've been talking about me to your friends then?"

"Maybe I keep a secret diary and wrote about you. The cops will find it when they search my flat for clues."

"Miss Bennett has quite the flair for the dramatic. Did she take acting lessons in school?"

"No. She just watched a lot of episodes of *CSI.*"

"Okay, I am getting the whole picture now. Meat, Sheppy's and Crime & Investigation Network. A nice eclectic mix you've got going for you . . . among other things." He said the last part very softly, the suggestion in the words hitting me directly between my legs. "So where do I collect you tomorrow after your photo shoot?"

"It's a studio shoot, so the Lorenzo Agency, tenth floor of the Shires Building."

"I'll find you, Brynne. Send me a text when you're finished and I'll be there. Good night." His voice changed, sounding more abrupt.

I heard a click and then nothing, realizing that Ethan had ended the call this time. Payback for earlier? Maybe. But as I got into my bed and rehashed our conversation in the dark, I became conscious of the fact he'd gotten his way again. I had a date with Ethan tomorrow night, and I'd never really agreed to go.

I sent the text to Ethan as Marco looked through the images. I'd worked with Marco one other time and I liked him a lot. Based in Milan, he liked classic poses reminiscent of the thirties and forties.

"You are magnificent in these, *bella*," Marco told me with that beautiful Italian purr. "The camera is your friend."

"It was nice. Thank you, Marco."

I still had to get ready and headed for the dressing room. I tried not to fuss over my appearance, but Ethan was so damned handsome. I was just . . . me. I knew I had a decent figure. I kept it that way, and my body was my livelihood at the moment, so I took care of myself. And I'd had plenty of attention from boys growing up. *Too much attention.* But I wasn't beautiful. I had long, straight, light brown hair, nothing special. My eyes were probably the most unique thing about me. The color was odd—sort of a mixture of brown, gray, blue and green. I'd never known what to put on my driver's license back home. I went with brown.

I opened my bag and slipped off my robe. Being it was nearly summer, and I assumed tonight would be casual at the end of a workday, I'd chosen clothes that would be forgiving of the time spent in a sports duffel— flax linen drawstring pants, a black, silky sleeveless top and black leather flats. I slung my favorite green cardigan over my shoulders and gave some attention to the rest of me. I brushed my hair out and went with a ponytail with a strand of hair wrapped around the elastic. Next, makeup, and it wouldn't take long. I rarely use much more than mascara and blush. Some lip gloss and a spray of my perfume finished me. *Good to go, Brynne.*

I pushed the call button at the elevators and waited. Ethan didn't say where to meet exactly, so I figured the lobby would be fine. He seemed to know the city like the back of his hand.

Marco walked up and gave me a hug in farewell. He was a demonstrative guy, always hugging and kissing on both cheeks in that Euro way that made it acceptable for him—and made the American me a sucker for it. I can admit to being fully charmed by the kind of courtly behavior rarely displayed in my native land.

I hugged him back and offered my cheek. Marco pressed his lips to my jaw right as the elevator doors opened and Ethan stepped out, glaring, his beautiful face set in a hard line.

I stumbled back from Marco's embrace and felt Ethan's hands catch me, latching onto my waist. "Brynne, darling, here you are." Ethan drew his arms up from my waist to wrap loosely around my shoulders, effectively pulling me away from Marco and right up against the front of his body. His very hard and muscled body. I could feel Ethan's stare on Marco and knew I needed to do something before the situation got more awkward than it already was. "Introduce us, Brynne," he said against my ear, the brush of his goatee pricking my jaw and making my knees weak.

"Ethan Blackstone, Marco Carvaletti, my—my photographer today." *Shit!* Did I really sound that fluttery and weak? I swear I was in deep trouble with this man. He got to me in a way I found so unnerving yet arousing at the same time; a tantalizing mixture screaming *Danger!* in my head.

Ethan held out his hand and offered a greeting to the tall Italian with the bemused expression at our situation. "How did my girl do today, Mr. Carvaletti?" Ethan drawled in his elegant voice.

Marco gave just the hint of a smile. "Brynne does her job to perfection, Mr. Blackstone. Always." The elevator dinged again and Marco stuck his arm out to hold it. "Are you going down?" Marco asked, stepping inside.

"Eventually. Not just yet," Ethan answered, settling a hand on both of my upper arms and holding me firm. We faced the elevator doors about to close. *Eventually?* I did not miss the suggestion in that comment. The image of his beautiful black hair moving slowly on his bobbing head between my legs was more than my libido could bear at the moment.

"Bye, Marco, thank you for the booking!" I managed to sputter, lifting a hand in a wave.

"Thank *you, bella,* the pictures are gorgeous as usual." Marco kissed two fingers and blew them at me as the elevator doors closed on him, leaving me securely in Ethan's grip and totally alone with the man who had an unmistakable erection pressed against my ass and the promise of knowing exactly how to use it.

"What are you doing!" I spat, spinning out of his hands. "What's with the 'my girl' and the territorial behavior, Ethan?" I turned to his beautiful face very aware that I was breathing heavy and with every inhale drawing more of his delicious scent inside me.

He came at me, backing me up against the wall in the corridor, his big body looming as he very deliberately lowered his mouth onto mine. Ethan's lips were soft in contrast to his goatee, and his tongue, like velvet, met mine in an instant; stroking over every part of my mouth, tangling with my tongue, sucking my bottom lip, getting inside me deep. As he pressed his big frame harder against me, I felt the solid length of his cock hit me in the belly. Ethan Blackstone took control of my body and I let him.

I moaned into his kisses and buried my hands in his hair. I brought him closer, my nipples tightening to brush against the chest muscles that felt so hard and male he had to be fiction. Except he wasn't fiction, he was kissing me passionately in a public hallway on the tenth floor of the Shires Building in front of the Lorenzo Agency. He'd come here to find *me*.

He held my face on both sides so I couldn't move away from the onslaught of his tongue. I was open to him and whatever he wanted me for. My reaction to Ethan was a weakness. I'd known it all along, even if only imaginary at first understanding. The real thing was devastating.

He moved a hand off my face and brought it down to rest on my neck. His kiss slowed to soft nibbles until he

pulled his lips away and I felt the cool air upon the wet-
ness he'd left there.

"Open your eyes," he told me. I lifted them to see
Ethan's face a mere inch away, his blue eyes burning hot
with lust.

"I'm not your girl, Ethan."

"You were during that kiss, Brynne." Eyes flickering, he
read me, and then he inhaled. I was a damp mess between
my legs, and I wondered if he could smell me. "You smell
so good . . . and fucking sexy."

Sweet Jesus! His thumb rubbed over my collarbone
where his hand still rested on my neck. And I did absolutely nothing to stop him. I was enjoying the view too
much. I'd tousled his hair from the mauling with my
hands. He still looked gorgeous and probably did even
when he crawled out of bed in the mornings. *Bed.* Was
there a bed in our immediate future? It would take next to
nothing on my part to get this man into bed. I didn't have
to be a genius to know he wanted sex. The real question
here was did *I* want it?

"Ethan." I pushed against the wall of steel that was his
body and got nowhere. "Why are you doing this? Why are
you acting this way toward me?"

"Don't know. I can't stay away and I'm not acting. I
tried to leave you alone but I can't do it." He feathered his
other hand over my hair and down until it was resting on
the other side of my neck. "I don't want to stay away from

you." He rubbed slow erotic circles with his thumbs meeting at the middle of my throat. "You want me too, Brynne, I know you do."

"How do you know that?" My voice came out in a whisper.

He brought his lips against mine again and kissed softly. "I can see it in your eyes and how you respond when I touch you."

I could hardly stand up on my own as he conquered me with more devastating kisses. The point was moot; I didn't need to stand. He had me braced against the wall at my back and his hips glued to my front. The elevator binged and he stepped back. I stumbled forward into his chest. He steadied me as a couple emerged and headed down the hall.

"We can't—we're in public. I don't do this sort of thing—I can't be here with you like th—"

He moved quickly, covering my lips with a few fingers to silence me and lifting my hand up to his mouth for a kiss. "I know," he said gently. "It's all right. Don't panic."

I could only stare spellbound as he pressed his soft lips against the back of my hand. The whiskers that framed his mouth brushed less softly but now felt nothing even close to the rough they had before.

Ethan looked at me with a measure of longing before taking the hand he'd just kissed and clasping it with one of his. He grabbed my duffel off the floor with his free hand and drew me into the open elevator. "Dinner first and then we can *talk* about things."

And in a way that was becoming very familiar whenever I was in Ethan's presence, I accepted that he'd completely taken charge again. He'd established control over everything, and had me right where he wanted.

Chapter 4

Vauxmoor's Bar & Grill was trendy but not boisterous to the point where we had to shout to talk. I mostly just enjoyed my view anyway. Seated over his plate of steak, Ethan was the picture of polite English gentleman. One supremely hot English gentleman. Gone was the heat and promise of sweaty sex we'd shared at the elevators. He'd turned that off just as quickly as he'd turned me on.

"How did an American find herself at university so far from home?"

I picked at my steak salad and went for a sip of cider instead. "I—I struggled for a bit after high school. I—" I closed my eyes for a moment. "I was a mess, actually, for a lot of reasons." Taking a breath to calm the nervousness that appeared whenever I had to answer this question, I said, "But with some *help* to focus my attentions, I discovered an interest in art. I applied to come here and by some miracle got accepted at U of L. And my parents were so thrilled to see me motivated they sent me off with hearty blessings. I have a great-aunt here—at Waltham Forest. My aunt Marie, but other than her, I am on my own."

"But you are taking a graduate degree now?" Ethan seemed genuinely interested in what I was doing here, so I kept talking.

"Well, when I finished my undergrad in art history, I decided to apply for advanced study in conservancy. They accepted me a second time." I stabbed a piece of steak with my fork.

"Any regrets? You seemed a little melancholy there when you were talking." Ethan's voice was soft when he wanted it to be.

I looked at his mouth and thought about what it'd felt like crushed against mine, forcing me to accept his kiss.

"About coming to London?" I shook my head at him. "Never. I love living here. In fact, I'll be devastated if I don't get a work visa when I finish my master's degree. I consider London my home now."

He smiled at me.

You're too damn beautiful for your own good, Ethan Blackstone.

"You do fit in here . . . very well. So well, in fact, I wouldn't have known you weren't native until you spoke, but even then, American twang and all, you blend right in."

"A twang, huh?"

"It's a very nice twang, Miss Bennett." He grinned across the table, his blues twinkling.

"So, what about you? How did Ethan Blackstone end up as CEO of Blackstone Security International, Ltd.?"

Still dressed for work in a fine dark gray suit that definitely cost more than my rent, he took a drink of his beer and licked the corner of his mouth.

"What's your story, Ethan? And you have a drawl, by the way, as opposed to a twang." I smirked at him.

One sexy eyebrow perked up. "I am the younger of two children. It was just my dad growing up for my sister and me. He drove a London cab and took me with him when I didn't have school."

"That's why you didn't need directions to find my flat," I said. "And I've heard about the test the London cabbies have to take on all the streets. It's gargantuan."

He smiled at me again. "That would be the Knowledge. Very good, Miss Bennett. For an American you are quite up on your cultural facts of Britain."

I shrugged. "I saw a show about it. Was pretty funny, actually." Realizing I'd distracted him from the conversation, I said, "Sorry for interrupting. So what did you do after you finished school?"

"I went into military training. Did that for six years. Left. Started my company with the help of contacts I'd made while enlisted." He looked at me longingly again, seeming to have no inclination to keep talking.

"What branch of the military?"

"British Army. Special Forces, mostly reconnaissance." He didn't offer any more details, but he grinned at me.

"You are not very forthcoming, Mr. Blackstone."

"If I tell you any more, I'd have to kill you, and that would just blow my promise all to shit."

"What promise?" I asked innocently.

"That I'm not a serial killer," he said as he popped a piece of steak into his beautiful mouth and started chewing.

"Thank the gods! The idea of eating a plate of beef with a serial killer would have totally *killed* this date for me."

He swallowed his meat and grinned at me. "Very funny, Miss Bennett. You are a wit."

"Why, thank you, Mr. Blackstone, I try very hard to be." He disarmed me with his charm so effortlessly that I really had to work to keep him on task. Ethan could turn a conversation to his advantage in an instant. "What do you do at your company?"

"Security mostly, for the British government and *some* private international patrons. Right now we are swamped with the Olympics. With so many people coming from all over into London—especially in our post-nine-eleven world—it's a challenge."

"I bet."

He pointed at my salad with his knife. "I bring you to the best place in town for a Mayfair steak, and what do you do?" He shook his head at me. "You order a salad."

I laughed. "It has some steak in it. Anyway, I can't help it. I don't like to be predictable."

"Well you're very good at being unpredictable, Miss Bennett." He winked at me and took another bite of his steak.

"Can I ask you a personal question, Ethan?"

"I get the feeling you're about to," he said dryly.

I sincerely wanted to know. The idea had been forming in my head for a couple days now. "So, do you—do you collect nudes . . . or something?" I looked down at my plate.

"No," he answered immediately, "I was working security for the Andersen gallery that night. There were a few high-profile guests, and I merely went to make an appearance. I have employees who do the actual on-site work." He paused. "But I'm very glad I attended, because I saw your portrait." His voice sounded amused. "I wanted it, so I bought it."

I could feel his eyes calling to me to look at him. I lifted my eyes up.

"And then you walked in, Brynne."

"Oh."

"I heard what you and Clarkson said, by the way—about me and my hand." He tapped his ear. "High-tech security gadgets in my line of work."

My fork dropped with a clang, and I must have jumped a foot. He smirked and looked smug, and far too sexy to be here with me. I was so mortified I wanted to run out the door. "I am so sorry you heard—"

"Don't be, Brynne. I try to avoid my hand to get off, especially if there are other, more lovely, options."

His fingers tugged on my chin. I felt my body heat up as I let him lift my face. *Whoa . . . breathe, Brynne, breathe.*

"Like you." He whispered the rest. "I want the real thing. I want you underneath me. I want to get off with *you.*" His blue eyes never left mine. He did not let go of my chin either. He held me firm and made me acknowledge his words.

"Why, Ethan?"

His thumb flicked out and brushed my jaw. "Why does anyone want anything? It's just how I react to you." His eyes rolled over me and got that smoky look in them. "Come home with me. Be with me tonight, Brynne. Let me show you."

"Okay." My heart pounded so hard I was sure he could hear it. And just like that I agreed to something I knew would be life-changing. For me, it would be.

The instant the word left my lips I witnessed Ethan close his eyes for just the briefest flicker. And then it was all a flurry of activity and purpose setting the pace from there; everything in sharp contrast to the sensual conversation we'd just been having. Within minutes he closed the bill from our dinner and led me out to his car. Ethan's firm touch pressed against my back, pushing me forward, taking me away to a place where he could have me. Alone.

Ethan drove us to a gorgeous glass building sitting high above the London skyline of previous centuries, modern but reminiscent of prewar Britain in an elegant way.

"Good evening, Mr. Blackstone." The uniformed doorman greeted Ethan and nodded politely toward me.

"Evening, Claude," he returned smoothly. The pressure of his hand, ever present on my back, propelled me forward into the open elevator. As soon as the doors closed us in he spun me and crushed his lips down on mine. It was just like the Shires Building all over again, and I felt the punch of arousal hit me hard between my thighs. And I was starting to get a clearer picture of my companion as well. Reserved in public, Ethan was all proper gentleman and restraint, but behind closed doors? Look. Out.

His hands were all over me this time. I didn't resist as he backed me into a corner. His touch warmed and made me soar both at once. He dragged his prickly whiskers down my neck and pushed his hand up my blouse to cup a breast. I gasped at the feel of his hot hands roaming as they made purposeful strides toward knowing my body. I arched into him, my chest thrusting out, pushing my breast further into his hand. He found my nipple through the lace and tugged.

"You're so fucking sexy, Brynne. I'm dying for you," he spoke against my neck, his breath tickling my flesh.

The elevator stopped and the doors opened to an elderly couple waiting to get on. They got one look at us and took a pass. I tried to push back from him, to put some space between our bodies. For the second time today, I found myself panting for Ethan like a harlot, out in the open for all and sundry to see me.

"Not here, please, Ethan."

His hand left my breast and reappeared from where it had been under my shirt. He brought it to rest on my neck. I felt his thumb start moving in a slow circle right under my chin. And then he smiled at me.

Ethan looked happy as he took my hand with his free one and brought it to his lips for a kiss. Damn, I loved when he did that.

"You're right, and I apologize. Do you forgive me, Miss Bennett? I am afraid you make me forget myself."

My belly flipped down low with an ache. I nodded at him because I couldn't do anything else, and whispered, "It's okay." The elevator, bless its mechanical heart, kept moving us closer to his floor. I wondered what he would do as soon as he got me inside his flat. Ethan had me totally under his spell, and I was pretty sure he knew it too.

Finally the elevator stopped at the top floor, and the soft settling made my belly roll again as Ethan put his hand on me. The man was tactile—always touching if he could get away with it.

He used his key to unlock the carved oak doors and pushed one open, ushering me into his private space. It was a beautiful room, lighter than I would expect for a man. The main room sported a gray and cream palette, lots of wood and moldings and decorative elements for such a modern space.

"This is beautiful, Ethan. Your home is lovely."

Ethan shrugged out of his suit jacket and tossed it over a couch. Taking my hand in his, he led me over to a wall of windows and a balcony that looked out onto the breathtaking city lights of London.

But then he turned me away from the view out the glass doors to face him, and took a few steps backward. He just stared at me for a moment.

"But nothing is as beautiful as you standing here, right now, in my house, in front of me." He shook his head, looking almost desperate. "Nothing compares."

I felt the overwhelming urge to cry for some reason. Ethan was so intense, and my poor brain was struggling to take everything in as he started moving toward me, slowly, like a predator. I'd seen the move before. He could go fast, slow, hard, gentle—*any* way, and make it look effortless.

My heart rate sped up as he came closer. When just inches from me, he stopped and waited. I had to lift my head to meet his eyes. So much taller than me, I could see his chest lifting with his own rapid breathing. It felt good to know he was as affected by this attraction as I was.

"I'm not beautiful like that . . . it's just the camera lens," I said.

He reached for my green sweater, undid the button, and slid it down my back until it landed with a soft swish on his shiny oak floor.

"You're wrong, Brynne. You're beautiful all the time." He went for the hem of my silky black shirt and drew it up over my head. I lifted my arms to help him.

In my black lace push-up bra I stood before him as he devoured me with passionate blue eyes. He brushed over my shoulders and traced over the swell of my breast with the back of his fingertips. The reverent touching made me ache for more, and I couldn't keep still any longer.

"Ethan . . ." I leaned forward into the stroking of his fingers.

"What, baby? What do you want?" He tilted my head to the side and exposed my neck. He kissed me there. The combination of his facial hair and those soft lips was electrifying. The pleasurable feelings grew to the point where I was totally lost to need. The point of no return had passed for me. I wanted him. Badly.

"I want—I want to touch you."

I brought my hands up to his white dress shirt and loosened his deep purple tie. He held me loosely and stared as I unknotted the silk, tight as a bowstring ready to snap. My fingers worked at the knot and in a minute I had his tie slipping loose to join my green sweater on the floor. I started unbuttoning his shirt.

He hissed when my fingers touched his exposed skin.

"Fuck, yes! Touch me."

I pushed his fine white shirt off him to the growing pile on the floor. I looked at his bare chest for the first time and nearly wept. Ethan was tight with muscles and washboard abs that melted into the most erotic V-cut I'd ever seen on a man.

I leaned forward and touched my lips to the middle of his chest. He put his hands on either side of my head and held me to him, like he would never let go. His strength and dominance were pretty clear. When it came to sex,

Ethan was the one in charge. And strangely, it soothed me to understand this. I was safe with him.

He moved down to kneeling, his hands sliding down my hips and then my legs. When he got to my shoes, he tugged at first one and then the other and removed them sweetly from my feet. His hands skimmed back up to the waist of my linen pants. He pulled the string and loosened the tie and then dragged them to the floor. He steadied my legs while I stepped out of the crumpled heap of linen, and then he kissed me right above the waistband of my panties. My belly fluttered some more and the ache between my legs got stronger. Ethan brought his fingers to the black lace and slipped them under the elastic. He drew downward and then they were off me.

He stared at my pussy, bare to his eyes, and he made a noise, very primal and very urgent, and then he looked up at my face again. "Brynne . . . you're so beautiful I can't— fuck, I can't wait—"

He feathered his fingers over my stomach and hips and pulled me forward to his lips and pressed them right on my bare mound. I shivered from the intimate touch that held me captive, waiting for what came next.

He stood back up and placed my hands deliberately on his waist. I got his message loud and clear. I started to work on his belt and then his slacks. He looked impressive. The ridge inside his boxers was impossible

to ignore as his pants came down. He growled when my hand brushed over the thin black silk covering his straining cock. As I bent down to focus my efforts on removing him from his clothes, he unhooked the clasp on the back of my bra and pulled it away. I was totally naked.

"I won't stay the night here, Ethan. Promise you'll take me home after."

He scooped me up and started carrying me out of the room. "I want you to stay with me. Once won't be enough—not with you." He kicked open a door and brought me into a bedroom. His face looked wild and desperate. "I need to fuck you first, and then I'll go slow. Give me tonight. Let me make love to you tonight, beautiful Brynne." He hovered over my face. "Please."

"But I can't stay the ni—"

His mouth swallowed my protests as he stretched me out on his soft, plush bed and started touching my body. Kissing my body. Heating my body until any conscious thought I had before this point fled my brain and kept on going. I was breaking my rules, and I was very aware of that fact as Ethan's tongue swirled over my hardened nipples, alternating between little scrapes of teeth followed by soft stroking to soothe what he'd done.

The contrast from the brush of whiskers on his goatee to the caress of his soft lips made me soar. I felt like I would orgasm just from what he was doing. The pleasure made me cry out and arch. My legs scissored as he worked on my breasts. Unable to keep still, I was wild and abandoned beneath him. He felt so good I couldn't regret this decision. All my reservations deferred to the exquisite workout he was giving my body and fled without another thought.

Being naked is not terrifying for me. I've done it a lot for the modeling and I know that men find my shape pleasing. It's the intimacy that is harder for me to process. So when Ethan says a thing like "Let me make love to you, beautiful Brynne," I knew I didn't have a chance.

"Ethan?" I cried out his name in abandon, not really for any other reason than to reassure myself I was in this with him and not off in some fantasy erotic dream world.

"I know, baby. Let me take care of you." He pulled back from my breasts, put his hands on the inside of my knees and opened me up. I was totally spread before him, and he stared down at my sex for the second time tonight. "Christ, you're beautiful . . . I want a taste of that."

And then he put his mouth on me. That soft tongue rolled over my clit and my folds and caressed. I could feel his goatee pricking the sensitive flesh as I writhed against his lips and tongue. I would come in a second and there was no stopping it. There was no stopping Ethan. He took what he wanted.

"I'm coming . . ."

"The first of many times, baby," he said from down between my legs.

And then two of his long fingers pushed their way inside me and started stroking. "You're tight," he rasped, "but when it's my cock in you, you'll be tighter, won't you, Brynne?" He kept finger-fucking me and flicking his tongue over my clit. "Won't you?" he asked again, this time more forceful.

I felt the rush, the tightening begin deep inside my belly as it started. "Yes!" I cried out in a push of air, knowing he expected an answer.

"Come for me, then. Come for me, Brynne!"

And I did, the experience unlike any other orgasm I'd ever had. I couldn't do anything else *but* come. Ethan pushed me to the edge and then caught me when I went over. I crested the wave of ecstasy pinned down with his fingers deep in my pussy, holding me there. It was shattering in its brilliance, and I could do nothing but accept what he gave me.

His fingers slipped out of me and I heard the sound of a packet being ripped open. I watched him roll the condom down his thick, beautiful, rigid cock. The part of him that would be deep inside me in a minute, and I shivered in expectation.

He lifted his blue eyes to mine and whispered, "Now, Brynne. Now I'm having you."

I sobbed inwardly at the image of him mounting me, the anticipation so great I was barely coherent.

Ethan loomed over me, the head of his penis tipped inside me already, burning hot and hard as bone. His hips forced me wider as he sank his cock down deep and true. He took my mouth, thrusting his tongue simultaneous in movement with his intrusion down low. I tasted myself on his tongue. I was taken by Ethan Blackstone in his bed. Totally and irrevocably.

I rode the wave as Ethan rode me. He did it hard at first. Pounding pulls in and out of my soaked core that went a little deeper on every stroke. I felt myself striving toward another orgasm.

The veins on his neck bulged as he propped himself up to get at me from another angle.

I squeezed my pussy around his pummeling cock while he worked me hard. He made all kinds of sounds and whispered dirty talk about how good it felt to fuck me. It just made me wilder.

"Ethan!" I shouted his name, coming a second time, my body in total surrender to his much larger and harder one as I shook and writhed in abandon.

He didn't stop. He kept on drilling me until it was his turn to orgasm. Neck straining, eyes burning, he took me harder still. I stretched to accommodate his length and girth as he grew a little tighter. I knew he was close.

I squeezed the walls of my vagina as forcefully as I had

ever done and felt him go rigid. Groaning out a guttural noise that sounded like a cross between my name and a war cry, Ethan shuddered over me with his blue eyes glowing in the dim of the room. He never took his eyes from mine when he came inside me.

Chapter 5

Ethan still kept his eyes on me. Even after we settled down from the rush of the sex, and after he'd left my body. He pulled off the condom, tied it and got rid of the evidence. But then he was right back, facing me again, his eyes moving over me, looking for my reaction to what we'd just done together.

"Are you all right?" he asked, brushing his thumb over my lips, tracing them ever so gently.

I smiled at him and answered in a slow voice, "Uh-huh."

"I'm not even close to being finished with you yet." He

dragged his hand down my neck, over a breast, across my hip to rest on my stomach. "That was—so amazing, I don't—I don't want this to be over." He left his hand splayed there and leaned forward to kiss me slowly and thoroughly, almost reverently. I could tell he was going to ask for something. "Are you—do you take birth control, Brynne?"

"Yes," I whispered against his lips. *I was right.* He would be surprised at the reason, but I wasn't sharing that information tonight.

"I want—I want to come inside you. I want to be here with nothing in between." He pressed his fingers into my slick folds and stroked back and forth. "Right here."

His words were a surprise, though. Most men didn't want to take the chance. My body reacted to his touch without volition, unable to keep from flexing toward his fingers. A sound of pleasure came from my throat.

"My corporation—regular medicals for everyone—we have to be fit, including me. I can show you the report, Brynne, I'm clean, I promise," he said, nuzzling at my neck and sliding long, purposeful fingers over my tingling clit.

"But what if I'm not?" I panted.

He frowned and stilled his hand. "How long has it been since you've . . . been with someone?"

I shrugged. "I don't know, a long time."

He narrowed his eyes just a fraction. "Like a week-long time, or months-long time?"

A week is so not a long time. Why I answered him, I have no idea other than it was part and parcel of what you got with Ethan. He demanded answers, he asked pointed questions, he just had a way about him that was nearly impossible for me to ignore when he probed into places I didn't want him to go. "Months" was my answer and as detailed as he would get from me right now.

His face relaxed. "So . . . is that a yes?" He rolled fully on top of me and trapped my hands intertwined with his, his knees splitting my legs wide open so he could settle in between them. "Because I want you again. I want *in* you again. I want to make you come with my cock so deep you'll never forget I was there. I want to come inside you, Brynne, and feel that with you."

I could feel him huge right now; hard, hot, probing me, and ready to sink in all the way. And as vulnerable as I was beneath him, in this moment I'd never felt more secure.

He kissed me deep, his tongue claiming me like before. It was a demonstration of what he wanted to do with his cock. I understood him very clearly most of the time. Ethan was not confusing in the slightest.

"I trust you, Ethan, and you won't get me pregnan—"

"Fuck . . . yeeees," he moaned on a thick slide of his bare cock against the still tingling walls of my sex. "Oh, baby, you feel so good. I'm—I am so fucking lost in you right now."

And that was how it went with him the second time. He moved slower this round, more controlled, like he wanted to savor the experience. It was no less satisfying either, because Ethan made me come until I was nothing but a limp vessel for his driving flesh.

He felt bigger inside me, harder, his balls slapping my drenched slit with every slide, and then he froze, his spine curving on a beautiful downward penetration that connected us so deeply I felt he was a part of me in that instant.

Ethan choked out my name and stayed buried just like he'd said he wanted to, and then a few, small, short jerks to milk everything from his tip until he stopped completely, breathing heavily and still between my legs.

He sucked lightly at my neck as I stroked over his back, the smooth muscles hot and damp with sweat. The room smelled like sex and whatever his delicious cologne was. I really needed to find out the name of it. I felt uneven ridges under my fingertips. Lots of them. Like scars? He shifted off me and my hands fell away. I knew better than to ask.

But he didn't go far. Ethan moved to his side and propped himself up and stared at me some more. "Thank you for that," he whispered, tracing my face with one fingertip, "and for trusting me." He smiled at me again. "I love that you're here in my bed."

"How long has it been since someone was in this bed with you, Ethan?" If he could ask, then so could I.

He grinned, looking very smug. "It's been since . . . never, my darling. I don't bring women here."

"Last I checked I was a woman."

He raked suggestive eyes over my body before answering. "Definitely a woman." He met my eyes. "But still, I don't bring *other* women here."

"Oh." I sat up against the headboard, pulling the sheet to my breasts. *How in the hell is that not a lie?* "That surprises me. I would think that you'd get more offers than you could possibly use."

He tugged the sheet down and revealed my breasts. "Don't destroy my view, please, and the operative word is *use*, my sweet. I don't care for being used, and women use men just as often as the other way round." He curled up beside me against the headboard and traced over a breast with one finger. "But I don't mind if you use me. You get a special pass."

I snorted and removed his hand. "You are far too handsome for your own good, Ethan—and you know it. That British charm will not get you a *free pass* with me on any day."

He made a sarcastic noise. "And you are one tough Yank. I thought I was going to have to pick you up and throw you in my car the other night."

"It's fortunate you didn't, or this nice shag we've just enjoyed? Never would've happened." I shook my head slowly with a smirk.

He tickled me at the ribs and made me squeal. "So it was just a nice shag for you, huh?"

"Ethan!" I batted his hands away and scrambled to the edge of the bed.

He dragged me back and pinned me beneath him, a huge grin on his face. "Brynne," he drawled.

And then he kissed me. Just slow and soft and gentle, but it felt intimate and special. Ethan settled me against his side and adjusted our bodies under the sheets, his heavy arm draped over and securing me. I felt myself grow sleepy in the warm bed with him. I knew it was a bad idea. Rules are rules and I was breaking them.

"I shouldn't stay the night, Ethan; I really need to go."

"No, no, no, I want you to stay," he insisted, speaking into my hair.

"But I shouldn't—"

"Shhhhhhh," he interrupted me like he had many times before and kissed my words away. He stroked over my head, trailing his fingers through my hair. I couldn't fight him. Not after tonight. The security felt too wonderful, my body too drained from all the orgasms, his hard strength too comfortable for me to battle him on the issue. So I slept.

The terrors are real. They come in the night when I sleep. I try to fight them, but they nearly always win. Everything is dark because my eyes are closed. But I hear the sounds. Cruel words about someone, disgusting words and names. And terrifying laughter . . . They think it's funny to degrade this person. My body feels heavy and weak. Still I hear them laughing and replaying all of the evil they have done.

I woke up screaming and alone in Ethan's bed. I figured out where I was when he came crashing into the bedroom, eyeballs wide. I started crying the minute I saw him. The sobs just got louder when he sat on the bed and grabbed me.

"It's okay—I've got you." He rocked me against his chest. Ethan was dressed and I was still naked in his bed. "You just had a bad dream, that's all."

"Where did you go?" I managed to ask in between gasps.

"I was just in my office—these fucking Olympics—I work at night lately . . ." He pressed his lips to my head. "I was right here the whole time until you fell asleep."

"You should have taken me home! I told you I wouldn't stay the night!" I struggled to get out of his arms.

"Christ, Brynne, what is the problem? It's two a.m. in the bloody morning. You are exhausted. Can't you just—why won't you sleep here?"

"I don't want it. It's too much! I can't do it, Ethan!" I pushed against his chest.

"Jesus Christ! You let me bring you to my house and fuck you wildly but you won't sleep in my bed for a few hours?" He brought his face down to mine. "Talk. Why are you scared here with me?"

He looked hurt and sounded more than a little offended. And I felt like a cruel bitch on top of being an
emotional, fucked-up mess. He also looked beautiful
in his faded jeans and soft gray T-shirt. His hair was all
mussed and he needed a shave around his goatee, but he
looked as devastatingly gorgeous as usual, even more so
because I was seeing the intimate Ethan, the one he did
not show in public.

I started crying again and telling him I was sorry. I really meant it too. I *was* sorry that parts of me were dam-
aged and broken but it didn't change the facts either.

"I'm not scared with you. It's so complicated, Ethan.
I'm—I am sorry!" I scrubbed at my face. "I want to go
home."

"Shhhhhhh . . . there's nothing to be sorry for. You just
had a bad dream, and I can't let you go home like this.
You're too upset." Ethan reached for a box of tissues beside the bed and handed it to me. "Do you want to talk
about it?"

"No," I managed to sputter through three tissues.

"That's fine, Brynne. When you feel comfortable you
can if you want to." His hand rubbing circles on my back
felt wonderful; I just didn't want to close my eyes again in
case I fell back to sleep. He pulled me down on the mat-
tress with him. "Let me hold you for a while?"

I nodded.

"I'll be right here until you fall asleep, and if you wake

and you don't see me, I'm just across the main room in my office. The light will be on. I would never leave you alone in my house. You're totally safe here with me. Security guy, remember?"

I grabbed more tissues and blew my nose, utterly wrecked and mortified at the situation. I did my best to bluff my way out of it, though, and I knew what I was going to do. I gave a soft laugh at his joke and let him tuck me back into his bed. I faced his chest and breathed in the scent I absolutely loved and tried to remember how beautiful it was. I focused on the feel of Ethan holding me safe, and the warmth of his big body. I tried to capture it all in my head, because I would not get this experience again.

I pretended to fall sleep.

I evened my breathing and faked it. And after a while I felt him slide off the bed and slip out of the room. I even heard the sound of his bare feet padding across the wooden floor. I watched the clock and gave it another five minutes before I got up.

I walked out into Ethan's living room buck-ass naked and scooped up my clothes. I removed his deep purple tie from the pile and smoothed it before draping it over the arm of his sofa, folded in half. I wished I could take it with me as a remembrance.

I got myself dressed quickly in front of the huge glass window and held my shoes in my hand rather than put them on my feet. I picked up my duffel and headed for the door. I could feel his semen wet between my legs, draining out, and the thought made me want to weep. Everything felt wrong now. I had ruined it.

Once I was out the front door, I ran for the elevator and pushed the call button. I shoved my shoes on my feet and dug around in my bag for a brush. I dragged that brush through my I've-just-been-fucking hair in brutal sweeps. The poor tangled mess didn't stand a chance, but it was better than nothing. The elevator arrived and I hopped on, stowing my brush and checking my wallet for cab fare as I descended.

When I emerged into the lobby the doorman greeted me. "May I assist you, madam?"

"Er . . . yes, Claude? I need to get home. Can you help me hire a cab?" I sounded desperate even to my ears. No telling what Claude might be thinking.

He did not show the slightest reaction, though, as he picked up a phone. "Ahhh, there we have one coming in now." Setting down the phone, Claude came around from behind his desk and held the lobby door open for me. He helped me to the cab and shut me in. I thanked him, gave the driver my address, and looked out the window.

The view into the elegant lobby was clear at night, so I could see when Ethan burst out of the elevators and spoke to Claude. He ran outside, but my cab was already in motion. He threw up his arms in frustration and rolled his head back. I could see his feet were still bare. I could see the look of confusion and hurt on his face when our eyes met—me inside the car and him on the street. I could see Ethan. And it was probably the last time I ever would.

Chapter 6

The glorious smell of coffee woke me up. I looked at my alarm clock and knew there would be no Waterloo Bridge run this morning. I came out to the kitchen with my arm over my eyes.

"Just how you like it, Bree, sweet and creamy." My sometime roommate and dear friend Gabrielle slid the mug in my direction, the expression on her face clearly readable. *Start spilling the dish, sister, and I won't hurt you.*

I love Gaby, but this thing with Ethan had so derailed me I just wanted to bury the knowledge of its existence and pretend he'd never happened.

I reached for the steaming mug and inhaled the delicious scent. It reminded me of him for some reason and I felt a bubble of emotion rise up strong. I sat down at the kitchen bar and crowded around my coffee mug like a mother hen protecting her chick. As I lowered onto the stool, the tenderness between my legs just served as another reminder. A reminder of Ethan and his hot body and model looks and the fabulous sex . . . and how I'd woken up in his bed hysterical. I gave up the joke of trying to be brave and let the tears come.

It took some time, two cups of coffee, and a move to the couch to get the story out of me. But Gaby is pretty good that way. She's relentless.

"I silenced your phone two hours ago. That duffel bag was making so much damn noise I wanted to kick it." Gabrielle stroked my head resting on her shoulder. "You've got voice mails and text messages up the wazoo. I think the poor thing was about to blow, so I saved it a cataclysmic death and shut the fucker off."

"Thank you, Gab. I'm so glad you're here this morning." And I meant that. She was like me in a lot of ways. A California native in London, studying conservancy and running from shit back home that haunted her. The only difference was that her father actually lived in London, so she was not totally on her own here in the UK. We'd found each other during that first week of classes nearly four years ago and never really let go. She knew my dark secrets and I knew hers.

"Me too." She patted me on the knee. "And you're going to make an appointment with Dr. Roswell, *and* make plans to go clubbing with Benny and me, *and* a stop into Charbonnel et Walker so we can gorge ourselves on sinfully rich chocolate." She tilted her head. "Sound good to you?"

"It sounds divine." I forced a smile and tried to pull myself together.

"And maybe you should give this guy a chance, Bree. He's good in the sack and he wants you bad."

I turned my fake smile into an authentic frown. "You've been gossiping with Ben."

She rolled her eyes at me. "Or at least call him back." Gaby lowered her voice to a whisper. "He doesn't know anything about your past."

"I know." And Gaby was right. Ethan didn't know about me.

Gaby rubbed my arm.

"I wasn't really mad or offended by him last night. I just had to get out of there. I woke up screaming in his bed and I—"

The urge to cry right now was just as strong as before. I tried to force the impulse down.

"But it sounds like he wanted to comfort you. He wasn't trying to push you away, Bree."

"But you should have seen his face when he burst into his bedroom with me howling like a lunatic. The way he

looked at me . . ." I rubbed my temples. "He's just so intense. I can't explain him properly to you, Gab. Ethan is
like nothing I have ever encountered, and I don't know if
I could survive him. If last night is any indication, then I
sincerely doubt it."

Gaby looked at me, her beautiful green eyes smiling
with confidence. "You are much stronger than you think
you are. I know this." She nodded firmly. "You are going
to go get ready for work, and then, after a productive day
in service to the great masterworks of the University of
London, you're coming home to get ready for our night of
decadent pleasures. Benny's already on board." She poked
me in the shoulder with her finger. "Now, move it, sister."

"I knew it. Ben outted me the instant he could." I smiled
at her, the first genuine smile I'd felt in twelve hours, and
heaved my ass off the sofa. "I'm on it, Gab," I said, rubbing
where she'd poked me. "I surrender."

I'd been at work for a few hours when Rory came through
the back with a vase of the most gorgeous deep purple
dahlias I had ever seen. He marched up to me with a beam-
ing smile on his face. "A delivery for you, Miss Brynne. You
have an admirer, it seems."

Oh shit! I did a double take. The bow on the vase was
not really a bow. It was his silk purple tie from last night.
Ethan had given his tie to me after all.

"Thank you for delivering them back here to me, Rory. They are gorgeous." My hand shook as I reached for the card on the plastic holder. I dropped it twice before I was able to read what he'd written.

Brynne,
Last night was a gift.
Please forgive me for not
hearing what you were trying
to tell me. I am so sorry.
Yours,
E

I read his note a few dozen times and wondered what to do.

How did he manage to confuse me so readily? One moment I felt sure I needed to flee Ethan, and the next I wanted to be with him again. I looked at my purple flowers once more and knew I most definitely needed to acknowledge his gift and that handwritten apology. To ignore them would be cruel.

Text or call? That was a hard decision. Part of me wanted to hear Ethan's voice, and another part was scared to hear mine when I tried to answer his questions. In the end, I went with a text and felt like a total wimp. I had to power up my phone first, and the barrage of missed calls and message alerts that flashed when it turned on made me ill without even listening or reading. It was too much for me at the moment, so I ignored everything and fired up a blank text screen: **Ethan, the flowers r beautiful. Ty. I ♥ purple.—Brynne**

As soon as I pressed send I contemplated turning my phone off, but of course I didn't. Curiosity killed the cat, or in my case, made me do stupid things.

I went over to the vase of my flowers instead and removed his tie from the arrangement. I put it up to my nose and inhaled. It had the smell. The sexy Ethan smell I adored. I was never giving this tie back to him. No matter what happened or what did not happen, the tie belonged to me now.

My phone lit up and started buzzing. My first instinct was to turn it off, but I'd known he'd call. And the selfish part of me wanted to hear him again. I put the phone up to my ear.

"Hi."

"Do you really love purple?"

The question made me smile. "Very much so. The flowers are beautiful, and I'm not returning your tie."

"I fucked up badly, didn't I?" His voice was soft and I could hear a rustling and then a breath exhaled.

"Are you smoking, Ethan?"

"Today more than usual."

"A vice . . . you have one." I traced over the tie spread out on my desktop.

"I have several, I am afraid." There was a moment of quiet, and I wondered if he considered me one of his vices, but then he spoke. "I wanted to come to your flat last night. I nearly did."

"It's good you didn't, Ethan. I needed to think, and that's very hard for me to do when you're close. And it's not anything you did last night. Not your fault. I—I needed some space after we were . . . together like that. It's just—it's just the reality of me. I am the one that's fucked up."

"Don't say that, Brynne. I know I didn't listen to you last night. You told me what you needed and I ignored you. I pushed too hard, too fast. I broke your trust, and that's what I regret the most. I'm deeply sorry—you have no idea how much. And if it ruins my chances of being with you, then I deserve it."

"No, you don't." My voice was just a whisper, and there was so much I wanted to say but did not have the expressible words to phrase it. "You don't want to be with me, Ethan."

"I *know* I do, beautiful Brynne." I could hear him exhaling from his cigarette. "And now the only question is, will you? Will you be with me again, Brynne Bennett?"

I couldn't help it. His words made me tear up. My only saving grace was that Ethan couldn't actually see me crying, but I was pretty sure he could hear me through the phone.

"And now I've made you cry. Is that good or bad, baby? Tell me, please, because I don't know." The yearning in his voice broke my resistance down.

"It's good." I laughed awkwardly. "And I don't know when. I have plans tonight with Benny and Gaby."

"I understand," he said.

Was I agreeing to see him again? We both knew the answer to his question. The thing is, Ethan drew me in. From the first night since we'd met he'd held me captivated. Yes, we had moved fast into sex. Yes, he had pushed me a little, but it had brought me to a place that felt wonderful, where I could forget about my past. Ethan made me feel very, very safe in a way that surprised me and forced me to consider the reasons for it. I didn't have a ton of faith that we might work out, but it sure as hell would be an affair to remember.

"Can we take it slow, Ethan Blackstone?"

"I'm taking that as a yes. And of course we can." I heard the soft brush of an exhale again. A pause as if he was gathering his courage. "Brynne?"

"Yes?"

"I am smiling so wide right now."

"I am too, Ethan."

Chapter 7

The club scene in London is pretty damn awesome. We didn't do it often, but a good club crawl was just what I needed. My poor psyche was on maximum overload in a conflict of emotions, fears and guilt. I needed to dance and drink and laugh, but most of all I needed to forget about all the shit. Life was too short to dwell on the dark parts, or at least that's what my therapist said. I had an appointment with Dr. Roswell the next day at four o'clock and a dinner date with Ethan after. Our first step in the take-it-slow agreement we'd made on the phone. He'd told me he wanted to lay the cards out on the table, and I have to admit I liked that. The truth works best for me. I really don't have anything to hide; it was more being careful about what I wanted to share. And I didn't know how much I could share with Ethan either. There was no guide map to help me. I had to ride the wave and hope I didn't crash into the reef and drown.

"Try this. It's magnificent." Benny handed me a tall orangey-red drink in a hurricane glass. "They're calling it an Olympic Flame."

I took a sip. "Nice." We both watched Gaby banging it out on the dance floor with some guy who would definitely *not* get lucky with her tonight. We'd hit three clubs so far, and my feet were starting to put up a protest. My dark purple boots looked great with my one-shouldered floral dress, but three clubs in and I was ready for some fluffy socks. "My cowboy boot fetish is coming back to haunt me, I think." I smirked at Benny and lifted a boot.

"You own like ten pairs of them." He shrugged. "I think they look hot. You know," he said thoughtfully, "nude in boots would make some delicious portraits." He nodded quickly. "Your body and your boots. Am I right? I want to do it. I can light it very dark and cast the boots in color. You have so many different shades—yellow, pink, green, blue, red. They'll look brilliant. Just art, nothing overt." He looked at me. "Will you do it, Bree?"

"Well, sure I will. If you think it'll make good pictures, then of course I'll sign a release for my boots." I stuck my tongue out at him. "My mother will have a coronary." I waited for Ben's sarcastic comment.

"Your mum needs a good rogering." Ben did not let me down.

I burst out in laughter at the absurd image of Clarice Huntington Bennett Exley ever being rogered at any time in her life.

"Hell, nobody ever said you had to have an orgasm to get pregnant, and I'm pretty sure my mom only had sex the one time with my dad."

"I think you could be right, my luv," Benny said. Ben had met my mom a couple of times, so he knew what he was talking about. "At least she got it right and made you if it was just the one time," Ben joked and I laughed some more.

My parents divorced when I was fourteen—probably from a lack of regular rogering and the realization that they had absolutely no interest in each other, but to be fair, they'd both stayed in the same general area until I'd graduated from high school. My mother would hop across the pond to London when the mood struck, and I would take great delight in shocking her with my friends, lifestyle and general obnoxiousness until she'd had enough of that particular visit. Her new husband, Frank, was much older than her, much richer than my father, and probably delighted when she left San Francisco on her trips. I doubt she got much rogering with Frank either. Maybe

Frank got some when she was traveling, but who the hell knew. My mother and I were at odds most of the time.

Now Daddy was a different story. He'd always been my go-to parent. He called me regularly and supported my choices. He loved me for who I was. And in my darkest hour was the sole reason I am still here walking the earth. I wondered what Daddy would think of Ethan.

Ben took off to chat up some hot blonde as a possible lay, and I stayed and sipped my Olympic Flame.

"Hey, lovely lady, those are some purty purple boots you got on there." A big guy with red hair, sporting his own pair of boots, western jeans, and a belt buckle in the shape and size of Texas loomed over my table. An American for sure. There were tons of people filtering into London for the Olympic Games, and this guy definitely looked like a European virgin.

"Thank you. I collect cowboy boots." I smiled at him.

"You collect cowboys, huh?" He dragged his eyes over me leeringly. "Then I s'pose I'm in the right place." He sat down next to me, his big body crowding me on the lounge seating. "I'll be your cowboy if you want," he muttered under his alcohol breath, "and you can ride me."

I scooted over on the seat and turned away.

"What's your name, sweetheart?"

"My name is I'm-not-interested." I stone-faced him. "And my middle name is You've-got-to-be-kidding-you-drunk-pig."

"Now, is that any way to be friendly to your American guests all the way here from Texas?" Big Red leaned closer and laid his arm on the back of the seat, pushing up against my side, his leg plastered next to mine, his breath blowing in my face. "You don't know what yer missin."

"I think I have a pretty good idea." I leaned back as far as I could from him and scooted further down the seat. "Do they teach you manners in Texas, or do the girls there like obnoxious drunks who proposition them in public?"

Big Red did not take the hint, or maybe he was too dumb to comprehend my question, because he grabbed my hand and lurched to his feet, pulling me along. "Dance with me, honey."

I balked, but his grip was so strong that I didn't have a chance against his tremendous mass. He was like a hairy red caveman who'd had too much grog, jerking me against his body and slithering us around the dance floor. His hand covered my ass and started creeping up my skirt. That's when I picked up my boot and rammed the heel down as hard as I could on his toe.

"Get your hand off my ass before your balls become pom-poms for my boots. You have two balls and I have two boots—one for each." I gave him a fake smile.

He grunted at me and narrowed his eyes. I could tell he was contemplating if I was serious or not, then he made a sneer and backed off of me. "Cold English bitch," he muttered, weaving through the crowd, off to harass some other poor person, most likely.

"I'm an American, you asshole! From the good part of the country!" I yelled at his back before spinning into the hard wall of a male chest. A chest I'd been up against before. A body that carried the scent of pure intoxication for me. *Ethan*.

He did not look happy as he scowled at the retreating bulk of Big Red and then back at me. Ethan pressed his hand to my back and pushed me toward a table. I could tell he was pissed. But even angry he still looked beautiful in his black T-shirt, dark jeans, gray jacket, and that wickedly serious glare on his face.

"Why are you here, Ethan?"

"It's a damn good thing I am, isn't it? That ape was all over you—his mitts on your ass—no telling what he would have tried next!" He glowered at me in the plush seat, his jaw a hard line, his lips set in a slash.

"I believe I handled him very well all on my own—"

Ethan took my face in his hands and kissed me, holding me trapped to his mouth, pushing his tongue in, demanding I allow him access. I moaned and kissed him back, tasting only mint and the faint taste of beer. I still couldn't believe he was a smoker. I could never smell it on him. Even if I'd wanted to deny his kiss, saying no to Ethan was next to impossible. I always wanted him. He pushed all the right buttons for me, and for that reason he was dangerous.

"Look at you," he said slowly, eyes raking down at my outfit and then back up to my face. "It's a miracle there aren't fifty hard-ons trying to get at you."

"Nope. Just two—Big Red and you."

"Who?" He narrowed his eyes.

It was my turn to raise a brow at him. "Benny was with me until a few minutes ago, and I'm gonna let that one slide. Not sure where to go with it." I folded my arms beneath my breasts. "Are you even supposed to be here, Ethan? Better yet, how did you know I was at this particular club? Are you stalking me now?"

He raked a hand through his hair and looked away from me. A bleached-blond cocktail waitress appeared instantly, blushing and jiggling as she took his drink order. I'm sure Miss-Sex-on-the-Beach wouldn't bat an eyelash if he asked her to sit on his lap. Seriously, how did he even come to a place like this without women stumbling at his feet?

When Ethan asked me if I wanted something from the bar I simply shook my head and lifted the drink Benny had bought me. The waitress gave me a look as she took off, hips swinging.

"What do I do for a living, Brynne?" His voice was steely, and I had to give him credit for not looking at her ass, considering she practically waved it at him like the Olympic flag, and the fact he was speaking toward the dance floor, sweeping the room with his eyes.

"You own Blackstone Security International, Ltd. and have the tools at your disposal to stalk your dates?" I said sarcastically, tilting my head in question.

He spun back to me and flicked his eyes over my body. "Oh, we're well past you being just a date, my beauty." He leaned in, his lips at my ear. "When we fucked in my bed you passed into uncharted territory—trust me on that one."

My heart stuttered at the look on his face and the words he'd just spoken. Instantly wet for him, I tried to steer the conversation away from the sexual. I don't know why I bothered, though; Ethan probably knew I was panting for him as we sat together.

"How did you know I was here?"

"Clarkson's credit card popped up. Only the work of a moment." He reached for my hand and caressed it with his thumb. "Don't be angry at me for coming. I would have just stayed back if you were with your friends, but that fucking cowboy put his hands on you." Ethan brought my hand up to his lips, the brush of his goatee a touch I was beginning to love and take for granted. "I wanted to see you having fun. You looked so sad the last time I saw you in that cab."

Ethan smiled and his whole face changed.

"I love when you do that," I said.

"Do what?"

"When you kiss my hand."

He looked down at my hand, still clasped in his. "It's

a very lovely hand, and I would be devastated if anything ever managed to harm it."

His eyes returned to mine again, but he mostly stayed quiet and watched me, rubbing circles with his thumb or pulling my hand up to his lips when he wanted to. Ethan needed to touch. It was just something he did that I understood about him. And oddly it comforted me. I couldn't explain it really, but I knew how he made me feel when he touched me. I suppose it was something I should discuss with Dr. Roswell at my next appointment.

Ethan's choice of words struck me as unusual, though. He was definitely overprotective, like he worried about me getting hurt. *That train pulled into the station six years ago, Ethan.*

Benny and Gaby showed up, did the meet and greet with Ethan, then slipped away about as inconspicuously as frat boys at a kegger thinking they were playing it cool. Whatever. I'm sure they would stay up half the night speculating anyway.

When his drink arrived he used his left hand to hold it. Ethan never let go of my right one. Not until he put me in his car to drive me home.

He kept looking over at me in my seat, pulling my eyes to his repeatedly, arousing me to the point where I felt the urge to squirm to relieve the ache between my legs.

"Why do you keep staring at me like that?" I finally asked.

"I think you know." His voice was soft with a hard edge to it.

"And I want you to tell me, because I really *don't* know."

"Brynne, I'm looking because I can't keep my eyes off you. I want to be in you. I want to fuck you so badly I can hardly drive the damn car right now. I want to come inside you and then do it again. I want your sweet cunt wrapped around my cock while you scream my name because I made you come. I want to keep you with me all fucking night long so I can take you over and over again and you don't remember anything else but me."

I gripped the armrest and shuddered, sure a mini orgasm just rolled through my body. My panties were so wet I could have slipped down the leather seat if my boot heels weren't dug into the carpet of the Rover.

By the time Ethan pulled up to the curb I was shaking. He got out and came around to open my door. He didn't say anything and neither did I. At the porch I fumbled for my key and dropped it. Ethan picked it up and got it in the lock and us into the foyer. He held my hand through five flights of stairs, neither of us saying a word.

I pushed open the door to my flat and Ethan followed me in. And like other times, the instant we were closed together in privacy, a different man emerged. A man barely contained in his hunger for me. I knew I would not say no either.

My back hit the wall and I was lifted off my feet in two

seconds. Ethan's mouth was on mine, probing and seeking two seconds after that.

"Wrap your legs around me," he said, tightening his grip on my ass.

I did what he told me to do. Spread against the wall, my purple cowboy boots dangling to the sides like the legs of a frog for dissection, I surrendered to whatever he had planned. I accepted that Ethan drove this part of us—the sex. He was in charge of every commanding thing he would do to my body, and I craved his touch far too much to have second thoughts right now.

"Unzip me and take out my cock."

I did that too. His hips pulled back to give me access, but his mouth and tongue still plundered as I unzipped his jeans and sprung him, hard as bone and sheathed in silk. I stroked his flesh with my hand as best I could and reveled in his guttural hiss at my touch.

Ethan got his hand up my skirt and his fingers under my thong. He ripped it up the back, snapping the material like a rubber band before impaling me on his enormous erection. I cried out as he filled me, so stretched by the size of him I convulsed from the sensation. He held me suspended for a moment, our bodies finally joined.

"Look at me and don't stop." He tightened his hands under my ass cheeks and started pumping into me. Hard. Deep. Punishing, really, but I didn't care. I wanted this from him as I stared into eyes burning blue fire at me.

"Ethan!" I moaned and writhed against the wall of my flat as he fucked into me, his cock owning me from the inside out. I kept my eyes on him. Even when I could feel the pressure start to build in my womb, and the tip of his penis hitting the deepest spot he could reach, I kept looking at him. The intimacy was off the charts and I could not have looked away if I'd wanted to. I needed my eyes wide open.

"Why am I doing this, Brynne?" he demanded.

"I don't know, Ethan." I could barely speak.

"Yes, you do. Say it, Brynne!" I tensed as an orgasm started to rule me, but he immediately reduced the pace, taking it down a notch with slow pulls in and out of my spread sex.

"Say what?" I cried, frustrated.

"Say the words I have to hear. Say the truth and I'll let you come." He speared into me slower and nipped at my bare shoulder with his teeth.

"What is the truth?" I was starting to sob now, completely at his mercy.

"The truth is," he grunted the rest on three, hard, punctuating thrusts, "You. Are. Mine!"

I inhaled on a cry at the final thrust.

He sped up again, fucking faster. "Say it!" he growled.

"I'm yours!"

The second I said the words his thumb found my clit and released the orgasm, rolling and crashing as hard as a powerful wave breaking onto the shore. Like a reward for obeying him. I cried through it, pinned to the wall of my flat, Ethan still going hard at me through the shearing pleasure.

A roar came from deep within his chest as he started to climax; the stare of his eyes was almost frightening. He thrust hard one final time, buried to the hilt as the hot seed pulsed up to soak me. He crushed his lips to mine and kissed, rocking the last few slides slow and gentle as he finished. His strong arms still held me up, and I don't know how he managed to do it but he did, kissing me sweetly and in total contrast to the sex-crazed madman of a moment ago.

"You are," he choked out, "mine!"

He set me down from the wall, holding me steady until my feet were solid, and then pulled out of my body, breathing hard. I leaned against the wall for support and watched him tuck himself back into his jeans and zip up. My dress fell back down. To anyone who walked in at this moment, there would be nothing to show we'd just fucked each other's brains out upon the wall. All an illusion.

Ethan put one hand up to my cheek, holding me captive, but gently, to face him. "Goodnight, my beautiful American girl. Sleep well and I'll see you tomorrow."

He brought his hand over my face, over my lips and chin and throat and down my front. The look of longing told me he didn't want to leave, but I knew he was going to. Ethan kissed me on the forehead so softly. He paused and inhaled like he was breathing me in, and then he walked out of my flat.

I stood there after the door closed, my body still humming from the orgasm, my ripped underwear up around my waist, the warm trickle of semen starting to flow down my thigh, and listened. The rap of footsteps following his retreat was a sound not to my liking. Not one bit.

Chapter 8

Dr. Roswell always writes in a notebook during our sessions. It seems very old-school to me, but then this is England and her office is in a building that was standing when Thomas Jefferson wrote the Declaration of Independence back in Philadelphia. She uses a fountain pen too, which impresses the holy hell out of me.

I watched her very beautiful turquoise and gold fountain pen scratch words into her notebook as she listened to me talk about Ethan. Dr. Roswell is a great listener. In fact, it's pretty much the gist of what she does. I don't know what our sessions would consist of if I didn't tell her stuff she could listen to.

Sitting behind her elegant French desk table, she was the picture of professionalism and genuine interest. I'd guess her to be in her early fifties with beautiful skin and white hair that did not age her one bit. She always wore unique jewelry and bohemian outfits that made her look cultured and approachable. My dad had helped me find her when I'd first moved to London. Dr. Roswell was on my necessities list along with food, clothing and shelter.

"So why do you think you reacted by leaving Ethan in the middle of the night?"

"I was afraid of him seeing me like that."

"But he did." She wrote something in her book. "And from what you've told me, he wanted to comfort you and for you to stay."

"I know, and it scared me. For him to want me to tell him why I have the dreams . . ." And this was my biggest problem. Dr. Roswell and I have discussed it many, many times. What would any man think of me once they knew? "He asked me if I wanted to talk about it. I told him no. He's so—so—intense; I know it will be a matter of days probably before he pushes for more."

"A relationship is like that, Brynne. You share and help the other person know about you, even the frightening parts."

"Ethan is not like that, though. He's so demanding *all* the time. He wants . . . everything from me."

"And how does that make you feel when he demands things or wants you to give him *everything*?"

"Terrified of what will become of *me*—Brynne." I took a deep breath and said the words. "But when I'm with him, when he touches me or when we're . . . intimate . . . I feel so safe and cherished, like nothing bad will happen to me with him. For whatever reason, I trust him, Dr. Roswell."

"Do you think starting a sexual relationship with Ethan is the reason your nightmares have resurfaced?"

"Yes." My voice came out tremulous, and I hated the sound of it.

"Brynne, that's a very normal thing for abuse survivors. The intimate act of sex is vulnerable for a woman by its nature. The female accepts the male inside her body. He's stronger and typically more dominant. A woman has to have trust in her partner or I imagine there would be minuscule few of us having any sex at all. Add that to your history and you have a very stirring mix brewing inside your subconscious."

"Even when you don't remember it?"

"Your brain remembers, Brynne. The fears of waking up to that betrayal are in there." She wrote another quick note. "Would you like to try a medication for sleep? We could see if that suppresses the night terrors."

"Will it work?" That sure got my attention. The suggestion of something as simple as a pill made me laugh nervously. The idea that I could stay with him all night . . . or he could stay with me . . . gave me some hope too. That is if Ethan still wanted to try sleeping with me. I remembered him walking out of my flat last night after the crazy sex-up-against-the-wall and how I'd not liked his leaving. My emotions were so confused. Part of me wanted him and part of me was terrified of him. I really had no idea what would become of us. *He made you tell him you were his.*

Dr. Roswell smiled at me. "We won't know until we try, my dear. Courage is the first step, and the drug is merely a tool to help you take more steps until you've made it down your path. Solutions don't have to be complicated every time." She reached for her prescription pad.

"Thank you so much—" My phone started vibrating in my purse. I checked it and saw the text from Ethan. "Ethan's here. He's in reception. We agreed for him to collect me at my appointment before he takes me to dinner. He said he wanted to talk about . . . us."

"It's always good for two people to talk about their relationship. The honesty and trust you give now will make it much easier to sort out your differences later." She handed me the prescription. "I'd love to meet him, Brynne."

"Right now?" Nerves began dancing in my belly.

"Why not? I'll walk you out and meet your Ethan. It helps me immensely to put faces to names when we have our sessions."

"Oh, okay," I said, getting up from her comfy, floral chintz chair, "but he's not really *my* Ethan, Dr. Roswell."

"We'll see," she said with a gentle pat on my shoulder.

My breath caught in my throat when I saw him looking at the art on the wall while waiting for me. The way he stood there reminded me of him seeing my portrait at Benny's show and wanting it. Wanting it enough to buy it.

Ethan turned when we walked into reception. His blue eyes lit up his face and morphed into a softened smile as he came toward me. A burst of relief shot down through my heart. Ethan looked very happy to see me.

"Ethan, this is my therapist, Dr. Roswell. Dr. Roswell, Ethan Blackstone, my—"

"Brynne's boyfriend," he interrupted me yet again. Ethan offered his hand to Dr. Roswell and probably gave her a smile that would melt her panties off. As they exchanged pleasantries I got a glimpse of her reaction to him, and I must admit it was satisfying to see women of all ages being intoxicated by his male beauty. And I would remember to use it during a future session too. *So, Dr. Roswell, you think Ethan is off-the-charts sexy, don't you?*

"Boyfriend?" I asked as he walked me out to his car, holding my hand firmly in his.

"Just keeping things positive, baby." He grinned and

pulled our entwined hands up to his mouth to lay a kiss on mine before putting me into his Rover.

"I can see that," I told him. "Where are you taking me and why do you look so smiley?"

He leaned over to my side and brought his mouth right up to my lips but didn't touch me. "I am always smiley, as you put it, when I get what I want." He kissed me chastely and pulled back.

"Since when do you *not* get what you want? You're the most demanding person I have ever met in my life." I tempered the sarcasm with a little smile of my own.

"Careful, baby. You have no idea of the depths of what I want to do with you." His eyes darkened.

I let that sensual threat float between us and tried to keep my breathing steady. "You scare me a little when you say stuff like that, Ethan."

"I know I do." He pulled my chin toward his mouth with a fingertip and kissed me again. This time he nibbled my bottom lip and teased it. "That's why we're taking it slow. I don't ever want to scare you." His eyes moved quickly back and forth as he tried to read me, his lips so close but not touching. "Do you realize this is our first time together where I didn't have to coerce you to come out with me? I have some hope, you see?" He gave me one last kiss before he pulled back to put the keys in the ignition. "And that, Miss Bennett, must be why I am smiley." His blue eyes danced now.

"Fair enough, Mr. Blackstone, I can live with that." He helped me click my seat belt and drove out of the parking lot. I settled back into the soft leather and breathed in his scent, allowing him to take me off to somewhere, and for the moment trusting that everything would be okay.

"Dr. Roswell seems very capable," Ethan said casually as he refilled my wine. "How long have you been her patient?"

I met his eyes and braced myself. *Here it comes, now how will you deal with it?* I told myself to breathe. "Nearly four years. Since I moved here."

"Did you go to see her today because of what's been happening with me?"

"If you mean going home with a complete stranger and letting him fuck me whenever we meet? Yeah, that's part of it." I took another gulp of wine.

His jaw ticked, but his expression did not change for the next question. "And leaving me in the middle of the night—is that part of it too?"

My head went down and I nodded. It was the best I could do.

"What hurt you, Brynne?" He asked the question so gently that I actually considered telling him for a second, but I was nowhere near ready.

I set down my fork and knew my shrimp fettuccini was finished. The topic of my past mixed with food is a definite no-go. "Something bad," I said, looking up again.

"I can tell. I saw your face when you woke up from your nightmare." He looked at my plate of food now pushed away and back up at me. "I'm sorry about that night. I didn't listen to you." He reached out for my hand and rubbed his thumb over the top of it. "I guess I just want you to know that you can trust me. I hope you know that you can. I want to be with you, Brynne."

"You want a relationship, don't you?" I stared down at his thumb rubbing over my knuckles. "You told Dr. Roswell you were my boyfriend."

"I did, yes. And I want you, Brynne. I do want a relationship." His voice got firmer. "Look at me."

I looked up immediately, his beauty so stark against the sea of white linens on the tables behind him. "Even with me the way I am, Ethan?"

"The way you are is perfect to me."

I removed my hand from his grasp. I had to tug a little to get him to let go. So very Ethan of him, wanting his way in all things, but he did allow me to turn his hand palm up and hold it. I traced over his life line and then his heart line and wondered if either of my lines was salvageable.

"I'm not, Ethan. Perfect and me don't belong in the same sentence." I spoke down to his hand.

"The proper phrasing should be perfect and I," he said knowingly. "And I totally disagree with you, my American beauty with the sexy twang."

I looked up at him again. "You are so controlling, but you do it in a way that makes me feel strangely . . . safe."

"I know that too. And it makes me fucking wild for you. And that's why you should trust me and let me take care of you. I know what you need, Brynne, and I can give it to you. I just want to know—I have to know that you want it. That you want to be with me."

The waiter arrived at the table. "Are you finished, ma'am?" he asked. Ethan looked annoyed when I told the server to take my plate and ordered a coffee.

"You hardly ate anything tonight." I could tell he wasn't pleased.

"I had enough. I'm not very hungry." I took a sip of wine. "So you want me to be your girlfriend, and give up control to you, and trust that you will not hurt me. Is that really what you want, Ethan?"

"Yes, Brynne, that's exactly what I want."

"But there's so much about me that you don't know. Things I don't know about you."

"When you're ready you'll share with me and I'll be right there to listen. I want to know everything about you, and if you want to know about me, you can ask."

"What if I don't want to give up control to you on some things, Ethan, or I am unable to?"

"Then you tell me. We are negotiating, and both of us have to respect limits."

"All right."

He tilted his head and spoke softly. "I want to be with you so badly right now. I want to take you home with me, and put you in my bed and have hours and hours with your body wrapped up in mine to do with as I wish. I want to have you there in the morning so when we wake up I can make you come, saying my name. I want to drive you to work and pick you up when it's time to leave. I want to go to the shops with you and buy food we can cook for dinner. I want to watch some crap television and have you fall asleep against me on the couch so I can watch you and hear you breathing."

"Oh, Ethan—"

My coffee arrived and I wanted to slap the server for interrupting that beautiful speech. I busied myself with doctoring it with sugar and cream. I took a sip and tried to find my words. To be honest, I was caught up in him already. Hook, line and sinker. I wanted all those things with Ethan, I just wasn't sure I would survive him.

"Too much? Am I scaring you off?"

I shook my head. "No. It sounds very nice, actually. And you should know it's something I've never had before. I've never had a relationship like that, Ethan."

He grinned. "That works for me, baby. I want to be your first." He raised an eyebrow in a look that dripped of sexual innuendo and made me want to go home with him tonight to start the arrangement. "But I want you to think about it tonight and then tell me what you decide.

And *you* need to know that I am very possessive of what belongs to me."

"Really?" The sarcasm rolled out of me. "Never would have guessed that from last night in my flat."

"I could totally spank your gorgeous arse right now for the lip you're giving me." He winked at me. "I can't help it. That's just how I feel about you, Brynne. In my head, you're mine, and that's how it's been since I first met you." He sighed across the table at me. "So I'm going to be restrained this time and take you home to sleep at your flat, and kiss you goodnight at the door, and wait for you to tell me otherwise." He signaled the server for the bill. "You ready to go?"

I giggled at the image that popped into my head.

"Are you laughing at me, Miss Bennett? Please do share."

"I am picturing you wanting to spank me, Mr. Blackstone, yet playing the restrained gentleman that merely kisses me goodnight at my door."

He groaned and shifted his legs in the chair, no doubt rearranging a furious hard-on. "You'll have witnessed a miracle tonight if my car actually manages to make it to your street."

Ethan kept his word. He did say goodnight at my door. Granted, he'd taken a few liberties with his hands and I'd gotten a very good impression of what he sported behind his fly, but he'd left me like he had promised after some very thorough kisses.

I got ready for bed after a hot shower and pulled on my softest sleeping tee. It had Jimi Hendrix on the front—the picture where he is in a garden at a table set for tea, considered the last photograph of him ever taken. I loved stuff like that, and I loved Jimi, so it got a lot of use.

Deciding it was time to do a little recon on my *boyfriend*, I fired up my laptop right in the middle of my bed and Googled the name I'd read on his driver's license when he'd showed it to me: *Ethan James Blackstone.*

Not a ton really came up for him. He had a Wikipedia page and some links for Blackstone Security's website. Wikipedia was a surprise, though. Ethan was known mostly for his celebrity as a poker player for high-limit games. He'd won a world tournament in Las Vegas about six years back at the impressive age of only twenty-six. A lot of money. Enough money to start a business. And with his military background in the Special Forces he must have found his niche. So that made him about thirty-two now. I did the math. Almost eight years older than me.

Google Images had some pictures of him, mostly of his big win at poker. I would have to ask my dad if he'd ever heard of Ethan. He loved poker tournaments and still played sometimes.

I kept scrolling through pages of images and stopped

whenever I found one of him. There was a picture of him with the prime minister and the Queen. *Jesus . . .* The Italian PM and the president of France? I felt tingles roll up my back. Was Ethan like a James Bond or something? What the hell kind of security did he do? If these were people he protected, then he had a *very* high-profile clientele. I was stunned. I made a note that the next time I saw Gabrielle's dad I would ask him if he'd heard of Ethan. He was London police, and if anybody was in the know, it was Rob Hargreave.

I'd also not seen a single personal photo of Ethan in a social situation with a woman. And I wondered if he held the power to squelch stuff like that. There was no way he lived a celibate lifestyle, not how he oozed sex. And if he was telling the truth about not bringing them to his home, then where did he take them for sex? Ugh, I didn't want to ponder the idea.

Shutting down my computer, I turned out the light and crawled into bed. I pulled his purple tie out from under my pillow and held it to my nose. The comforting scent of him came to me instantly. I felt even smaller in the scheme of things now. And was left wondering why a man like him had noticed me in the first place. From just my portrait at a gallery show? The idea hardly seemed believable.

I tried to conquer my fears and think about what he'd offered to me tonight. And I remembered how good it felt to be with him and how he made my body burn during sex. I didn't have to worry about anything scary or underhanded with Ethan. He was, if nothing else, brutally honest. He was dominating, sure. But I liked that. It took the pressure off me in a sector of my life where I held little confidence. I wanted him, I just didn't know if he would want me once he knew my whole story.

Chapter 9

Waterloo Bridge grounded me the next morning. I came home to the heavenly smell of coffee started by my roommate. I passed Gaby a half hour later on my way out the door to class.

"You going to the Mallerton Gala on the tenth?" she asked.

"I want to. I'm conserving one of his right now, called *Lady Percival*. I was hoping to find out a little more about the provenance on her. She's had some heat damage, and it's melted the lacquer over the title of the book she's holding. I really want to know what that book is. Like a secret I need to discover."

"Yay!" She clapped and did a little bounce. "It's his birthday exhibit."

I pretended to count on my fingers. "Let's see, Sir Tristan would be two hundred twenty-eight?"

"Two hundred twenty-seven, to be exact." Gabrielle was deep into her dissertation on Romanticist painter Tristan Mallerton, so when there was anything doing with him she was first in line with tickets.

"Okay, off by one year. That's not too bad."

She smiled wide, revealing perfect white teeth and full lips that made me wonder why she wasn't the model. The reddish glints in her dark hair, combined with her slightly olive complexion, made her look exotic. Men were always tripping over my roommate, but she wanted nothing to do with them. A lot like me, I thought. Until Ethan came along and upset my cozy existence.

"Let's plan to go together—make a night of it. I want a new dress, though. You wanna set up a shopping expedition too?" Gaby looked and sounded too damn excited for me to say no.

"Sounds excellent, Gab. I need some distractions from my suddenly more complicated life." I tilted my head and mouthed the word *"Ethan."*

Gaby gave me the once-over and crossed her arms. "What happened with you two?"

"He wants a relationship. Like a real one where we sleep over and cook dinner and watch TV."

"And lots and lots of hot orgasmic sex," Gaby added and then held out her arms to me. "Come here. You look like you need a hug."

I went into her embrace and held on tightly to my friend. "I'm scared, Gab," I whispered at her ear.

"I know, sweetie. But I've seen you with him. I've seen how he looks at you. Maybe this is the big one. You won't know unless you try." She touched my face. "I'm happy for you, and I think you've got to go with a little leap of faith here. So far Mr. Blackstone is on my good list. If that should change or if he hurts one smooth hair on your innocent head, then his pretty-boy balls are gonna be transformed into a set of Klik Klaks. And please tell him I said that."

"God, I love you, woman!" I laughed and headed off to class, thinking about how I would break the news to Ethan.

Three hours later he sent a text: **Ethan Blackstone: <---misses Brynne. When will I see u?**

I smiled as I read the words. He missed me and he wasn't afraid to say it. Ethan's direct approach did wonders toward calming my nerves and fears about a relationship together, I must admit. I gathered my resolve and replied: **Brynne Bennett: <--- is :) Very soon if ur not 2 busy. Can I come 2 ur office?**

My phone lit up almost immediately with an emphatic *YES*, along with instructions of where to go, elevator to take, plans to feed me lunch—typical modus operandi for my Ethan. That made me smile too. *Did I just say* my *Ethan?* I so did, I realized as I ducked into the Underground station and began descending stairs.

I wanted to stop at a pharmacy to get my new prescription filled along the way, so I hopped off the Tube two stations later. Heading back up to the street, I entered a Boots and dropped off the prescription. I grabbed a shopping basket and browsed while I waited for the pharmacist to fill it. An idea formed in my mind and I went with it, plucking items from the shelves and dropping them into my basket.

In the checkout line to pay, I noticed a big guy behind me waiting with his lone bottle of water. Well, I really noticed his tattoo. He had a beauty on the inside of his forearm—a perfect rendition of Jimi Hendrix's signature, the big swirl of the *J* as clear as if Jimi had scrawled it himself. "Nice tat," I said to him, noticing how really huge he was. At least six five, solid muscle, with spiked white-blond hair and a face that exuded confidence—this was a guy you did not mess with.

"Thank you." His nearly black eyes softened just a bit and he asked, "Are you a fan?"

His British accent soothed me for some reason, again totally at odds with his physical appearance. "Massive fan," I answered with a smile before heading out to get back on the Tube.

I plugged into my iPod on the train. Might as well listen to some Jimi and think about what to tell Ethan when I saw him.

Blackstone Security was in Bishopsgate at the center of old London with all of the other modern skyscrapers. Somehow this was not a surprise to me as I tried to picture Ethan behind a desk—in a sexy suit—and smelling delicious. I exited the Tube at the Liverpool Street station and started up the stairs to the sidewalk. I stumbled on a crack in the concrete step and grasped for the handrail. My knees were spared but my shopping bag dumped out, contents scattering. I muttered a curse as I turned to bend down to retrieve everything and faced the same guy I'd seen in line at Boots with the Hendrix tat.

He efficiently helped me with my stuff and handed the bag to me. "Watch your step," he said softly and continued on up the stairs.

"Thank you," I called to his retreating back, where muscles rippled under a black dress shirt. I'd barely made it out to the sidewalk when my phone started buzzing: **Ethan Blackstone: <--- is worried. Where r u?**

I had to smile at his attention to detail . . . like time allotments. I sent back: **Brynne Bennett: <--- is almost there. Patience!!!!**

The marquee in the lobby listed Blackstone Security International on floors forty through forty-four, but Ethan had told me to find him on the forty-fourth. I walked up to security and gave my name. The guard smiled slightly and handed me a pen to sign in. "Mr. Blackstone is expecting you, Miss Bennett. If you'll just step this way, I'll create your badge so you may just scan through on future visits."

"Oh, all right." I let the man do his job, and within minutes I was gliding up to the forty-fourth floor sporting my own Blackstone Security ID badge. My heart pounded a little faster the closer I got to my destination. I swallowed a few times and rearranged my black leather jacket. The black skirt and red boots paired with it were not slum wear by any stretch of the imagination, but I wasn't dressed for a business office either. I felt suddenly self-conscious and hoped people didn't stare at me. I hate that.

With my purse on my shoulder and my Boots shopping bag in my hand, I stepped out of the elevator and walked into a very sleek and artfully designed space. There were framed black-and-white photographs of architectural wonders from all over the world on the walls, big glass windows looking out over the city, and a very pretty redhead behind the desk.

"Brynne Bennett here to see Mr. Blackstone."

She looked me over thoroughly before getting up from her desk. "Oh, he's expecting you, Miss Bennett. I'll take you back through to his office." She smiled as she held the door for me. "I hope you like Chinese."

I followed her and dismissed the comment, not because I didn't want to answer but because everyone was watching us. Every head at every workstation turned in our direction and stared. I wanted to sink through a crack in the floor and hide. That would be after I killed Ethan. What the hell had he done? Announced in a mass email that his *girlfriend* was stopping by to give him a blow job at his desk? I felt my face heat up as I followed the cute receptionist, who did indeed have an engagement ring on her left hand. I probably noticed only because I refused to look up at all those faces. "Wow, quite a welcome wagon you've got here," I muttered.

"Don't worry, they're just curious to see who's got the boss's attention is all. I'm Elaina, by the way."

"Brynne," I said. She stopped and knocked on a magnificent set of ebony double doors before entering.

"And this is Frances, Mr. Blackstone's assistant. Frances, Miss Bennett has arrived."

"Thank you, Elaina," Frances smiled and addressed me. "Miss Bennett, it is a pleasure to meet you." She extended her hand and shook firmly. I wondered if it was very bad to love the fact that Ethan's personal assistant was probably older than my mother and a fan of polyester suits. My insecurity meter shot down a few notches as I smiled back at Frances. Still, she was kind and confident as the ruler of her domain when she pointed to the second set of doors. "Please go on in, dear. He's been waiting for you."

I opened the heavy-looking door that moved so smoothly my pinky could have pushed it, then fled inside to Ethan's office. I shut the thing and collapsed against it, seeking him with my eyes closed and finding him with my nose.

"That's right. Keep on with what you're doing. Yes. I want hourly reports when you're in the field. Protocol." He was on the phone with somebody. I opened my eyes and watched him from my post against his office door. So confident and beautiful in his dark gray pinstripe. And lo and behold, another purple tie! This one so dark it was nearly black, but man did it look good on him. He ended the call and looked over at me. I felt the door click against my back. He grinned with one eyebrow up. I glared back at him.

"All those people staring at me, Ethan! What did you do, send an email to the whole frickin' office?"

"Come over here and sit on my lap." He pushed back from his big desk and made room for me. No reaction to my accusation whatsoever. Just a confident demand out of that beautiful mouth that I come over to him immediately.

Well, I did it. I marched my red boots over to him and plopped down as ordered. He put his arms around me and tugged me into his body for a kiss. It helped my mood considerably.

"I might have let it slip to a few that you were coming to see me." He pushed a hand up my thigh and under my skirt, his temperature hot to my feeling. "Don't be mad at me. You took forever to get here, and I had to keep checking up front with Elaina to see if you'd arrived."

"Ethan, what are you doing?" I murmured against his lips as his hand kept trailing those long fingers toward their destination. He forced my legs to part so he could get up in between them to my pussy.

"Just touching what's mine, baby." He traced my folds through the red lace panties I'd worn and then pushed the material aside.

I flexed my muscles in anticipation and panted harder. "How many times did you go out to check for me?"

"Only a few . . . four or five." His finger found my clit and starting rubbing circles over the now slick bundle of nerves, making me incoherent as usual.

"That's a lot of times, Ethan . . ." I barely got the words out, I was so captured by the pleasure going on from his magic fingers. I opened my legs a little wider and rode his hand. "The door—"

"—is locked, baby. Don't think about anything but me and what I'm doing." Ethan gripped me hard with one hand and captive with the other. There was nothing for me to do but focus on where he was taking me. He switched to his thumb and rubbed a little harder. Two fingers entered on a slick slide and started stroking. "You're so fucking wet for me." He slammed his mouth onto mine and claimed that too.

I cried out as I came atop Ethan's lap with his fingers

inside me and his tongue in my mouth, totally overcome and dominated. And very satisfied. He held me firmly, like he was afraid I would try to leave, but he needn't have worried.

I breathed deeply, the sensations still filtering through my bloodstream as I tried to process his effect on me. I had no self-control around Ethan. None.

I looked at him when I could manage it and got drilled by those incredibly blue eyes of his. "Your hand must be a mess," I said, knowing what he'd said was true. I *was* soaking wet.

He grinned naughtily and wiggled his fingers still in me. "I love precisely where my hand is right now. I wish it was this, though." He thrust his cock up against my ass, and I didn't doubt he did. I could feel how hard he was and shivered.

"But—we're in—it's your office."

"I know, but that door is locked and nobody can see in here. We're totally private." He nuzzled my neck and whispered, "Just you and me."

I moved to get off him but he held me firm, a flicker of displeasure crossing his eyes. I tried again and he let me go this time. I slid to the floor to my knees and faced his crotch, my body mostly hidden behind his desk. I put my hands over his erection and pressed. I looked up at him and saw the look of want and desire in his eyes and knew what I needed to do. "Ethan, I want to suck—"

"Yes!" It was all the direction I needed. I unbuckled and unzipped and uncovered my prize. God, he had a beautiful penis. Ethan hissed when I took him in hand and licked the tip, loving the salty taste of his flesh. I pulled back and looked some more. This thing had been inside me—a few times—and I'd never really gotten a good look. He was big and hard and smooth as velvet. I stroked him up the length and smiled up at him. He was biting his lip and staring down at me like he could snap in two with the slightest pressure.

"You're perfect," I murmured, and then I closed my mouth over him and drew his beautiful pink cock into me. Ethan gripped the chair and thrust to the back of my throat. I worked him good, stroking with my hand and sucking him deep into my mouth. With my tongue, I flicked over the big vein that fed his erection and heard him groan. I didn't stop my pace or where I was going with this. It would be all-the-way-to-the-finish-line with me, and I intended to get my way.

He must have read my body language, because his hands moved to my head and held me as he fucked my mouth. I took it all without gagging once, and when his balls tightened up and I knew he was close, I gripped his hips hard with both hands so he couldn't pull back.

"Oh, fuck, I'm gonna go so hard!" He stiffened to iron and spilled the warm essence down the back of my throat, holding my head with two hands as he climaxed.

"Jesus Christ, Brynne." He panted out deep, gulping breaths.

I lifted my eyes when he left my mouth. I swallowed slowly and saw his bottom lip tremble as he watched. He pulled me toward him, up from the floor, both hands still holding the sides of my face, and kissed me slow and deep and so sweetly that I soared at the gesture. I was glad to have pleasured him. It made me happy to make him happy.

Back on his lap again after restoring our clothes, we got comfortable and sat in his chair together. He trailed his fingers in my hair and nibbled at my neck. I played with his engraved silver tie clip that looked like something vintage and just let him hold me for a bit. "This is beautiful," I told him.

"You're beautiful," he whispered against my ear.

"I love your office. The photographs in reception are gorgeous."

"I love it when you visit me at my office."

"I can see that, Ethan. You are quite . . . welcoming." I giggled at him. He tickled me and let me squirm for a little too long, in my opinion. I smacked his hands away from my ribs.

"What did you bring me from your shopping? I hope it's a sweet," he said, reaching for the Boots bag. "I like Jolly Ranchers. Cherry is my favorite—"

I grabbed the bag from him before he could look. "Hey!

Don't you know better than to dig through ladies' bags? You might find something to embarrass us both in there."

He pursed his lips together and sighed. "I suppose you could be right," he said far too easily. Then he grinned like a demon and snatched the bag completely out of my hands. "But I want to look anyway!" He held it out of my reach and started pulling out items. He got quiet when he extracted the purple toothbrush and then a tube of tooth-paste. He set them on his desk and put his hand back into the bag. Out came a new hairbrush, some moisturizer and the lip gloss that I use. He kept bringing out all the stuff I'd bought at Boots. My brand of shampoo, shaving gel, and even a small bottle of Tommy Hilfiger's Dreaming fin-ished off the toiletries. He lined everything up neatly and looked at me very still and very serious. "But I thought you couldn't, Brynne."

"Me too." I took out the one thing he had left in the bag. My prescription. "But Dr. Roswell gave me this, and some hope that I can do it." I touched his hair and smoothed it. "They're pills to help me sleep so I won't wake up like I did last time. I mean, if I'm your girlfriend, then I want to . . . try to stay over with you sometim—"

He cut me off with a kiss before I could say any more.

"Oh, baby, you've made me so happy," he told me be-tween more kisses. "Tonight? You'll stay tonight? Please say yes." His expression told me all I really needed to know. He wanted me to stay, fucked-up sleeping habits and all.

I looked down at his tie clip again and spoke to that. "If you're willing to try it and so am I, then how can I say no?"

"Look at me, Brynne."

I did and saw the hard set of his jaw behind the goatee. I could see lots of emotion in him too. Ethan did not really hide it from me ever. He might be reserved in public, but in private with me, he wore his heart on his sleeve. What you saw was what you got. He told me what he wanted from me with no apology for how blunt the words were.

"I want you to see it in my eyes when I say that I am so willing to try, and so happy that you are too." He kissed my hair. "And I want you to pick a word. Something you can say to me if you need some space because you're scared or if I do something you don't want to happen." He held my face to his. "You just say the word and I'll stop, or I'll take you home. Just please don't ever walk out like that again."

"Like a safe word?" I asked.

He nodded. "Yes. Exactly like that. I need you to trust me. I need that, Brynne. But I need to trust you too. I can't—I don't want to feel like that again. When you left me that night—" He swallowed hard. I saw the movement of his throat pulsing and knew this was something important to him. "—I don't want to feel how I felt when you were gone and I knew I couldn't come to you."

"I'm sorry I left you like I did. I was overwhelmed by you. You overwhelm me, Ethan. You need to know that because it is the truth."

He pressed his lips to my forehead and spoke. "Okay, but just tell me when. Say your word, whatever, and I'll back off. Just don't leave me like that again."

"Waterloo."

He looked at me and smiled. "Waterloo is your safe word?"

I nodded. "That's it." I looked over at the food set out on the table for our lunch and inhaled. Chinese, from what Elaina had said, my nose agreeing. "Are you going to feed me or what? I thought I was getting lunch out of this deal." I poked him in the chest. "A girl needs more than just an orgasm, you know."

Ethan threw his head back and laughed and delivered a firm smack to my ass. "Off you go then. Let's get you fed, my beautiful American girl. We have to keep you in top form. I have big plans for you tonight."

He flashed me a wicked wink. I knew I was lost.

Chapter 10

My phone rang as I was packing my overnight bag. I saw who was calling and looked at the clock. Ethan had said he would be here by seven to pick me up. It was quarter to right now. "Are you having second thoughts and crying off for our sleepover tonight?"

He laughed. "No chance of that, and I hope you have your bag ready, baby."

"So why aren't you here to whisk me away?"

"Yes, well I had to send a car to collect you. Some business-related emergency pain in my arse. I'm so sorry. The driver's name is Neil, and he works for me. He'll get you into my flat and I want you to just make yourself at home until I get there. Will you do that for me, my darling?"

"I guess so." My mind was spinning with the implications of me on my own in his house. I wasn't really scared, but the idea did not thrill me either. "Are you sure, Ethan? I mean—we can do this another night if you're busy—"

"—I'm sleeping with you tonight, Brynne. In my bed. End of discussion."

"Oh boy." I smiled into the phone. "Can I start dinner for you, then? Is there food in the house, or should I have your driver stop at the market?"

"No need to stop. There's food and even some things in the freezer. My housekeeper cooks meals and freezes them. You choose whatever you like—excuse me." I heard muffled voices and Ethan speaking to someone. "I have to go, baby. I'll see you as soon as I can get there."

I said good-bye, but he was already off. I stared at my phone for a moment before setting it down, lost in the surreal, and feeling like Alice in Wonderland again. My life seemed to be careening in fast-forward with me unable to switch modes. I'd gone from single girl to girlfriend in just over a week with no sign of a slowdown. At all.

My phone lit up again with no screen ID on display. "Hello?" I answered.

"Ma'am, my name is Neil McManus. Mr. Blackstone instructed me to pick you up. There's a black Rover waiting down at the curb for you now." The smooth English accent formed the words efficiently.

Neil. I remembered what Ethan had said about the driver. "Sure. Be right down." I slung my bag over my shoulder and made it out to the street at a quick clip. The car that waited looked exactly like Ethan's Range Rover, but I skidded to a halt when I got a load of Neil-the-driver; huge, muscular, bleached blond, spike-haired with very dark eyes.

"You!" I said, completely shocked. It was the guy with the Jimi Hendrix tat from today.

"Yes, ma'am." He held open the passenger door for me, his expression giving away nothing.

"You were following me around today!" It was no question, as I am sure Neil realized. I dropped my bag to the ground, folded my arms beneath my breasts and went for a Mexican standoff instead. "Give me one good reason why I should get in that car with you, *Neil*."

Neil smiled briefly and looked down to my bag on the sidewalk. "I work for Mr. Blackstone?"

I gave Neil my best stone face.

He tried again. "He will fire my arse if I don't get you delivered to his flat per his instructions?" He looked back up at me, his dark eyes sincere. "I very much like my job, ma'am."

My head started spinning with more wild thoughts of what I was doing, what Ethan was up to, how many people were involved in my business, and my list could have gone on and on. Man, oh man, did we need to have a discussion or what! Still, it wasn't fair to take out my frustrations on Neil, who for all appearances was just doing his job.

"Fair enough, Neil." I picked up my bag and got in the backseat. "But the deal's off if you keep calling me ma'am, got it? My name is Brynne. And if *Mr.* Blackstone doesn't like it, you can tell him that he can kiss my informal Yankee ass. He should know that American girls despise being called ma'am!"

Neil tilted his head at me and cracked a grin as he shut my door.

He started driving as I seethed in the backseat. The silence just irritated me, so I figured I might as well get it all out in the open. "So Ethan hired you to stalk me around London, huh?"

"Protection, ma'am . . . ahhh . . . Brynne. Not stalking you," Neil answered.

"Protection from what?" I demanded. "Are you watching when I go for my runs in the mornings too?"

Neil looked up at me through the rearview mirror. "The city can be a dangerous place." His eyes went back to the road. It had started to rain, and the buzz of the windshield wipers dragged rhythmically back and forth. "He's just very watchful, is all," Neil said quietly.

"Yeah, I know." Ethan is watchful and controlling and more than a little high on the arrogant scale for my tastes much of the time. He was so in trouble with me. "So how long have you worked for him, Neil? Ethan tells me absolutely nothing, so I figure you can enlighten me." I smirked into the rearview for his benefit.

"Six years now. We were in the SF together."

"That's Special Forces, right? So are you guys some kind of James Bond for the British government?"

Neil actually laughed and shook his head. "I can see why Mr. Blackstone keeps a watchful eye over you, Brynne. You have quite the imagination."

"Yeah, Ethan's told me that one too," I said dryly.

As annoyed as I was with Ethan's presumptions—which were well beyond out of line—I couldn't really take it out on Neil. He seemed like a decent guy, and he had great taste in music. I liked him. Neil was simply doing his job. Whatever that was in regards to me.

Neil got the car parked and us into the elevator through the garage entrance. Before I knew it, I was inside Ethan's gorgeous home again, just this time, without Ethan.

Neil had me put his number into my cell and said he would be close if I needed anything. "How close is close? Am I private here? You can't watch me in his house, can you?" I checked his eyes for telltale signs of subterfuge. "Do not even think about lying to me, Neil. I will be out that door so fast Ethan will feel the wind ruffle his hair all the way from here to wherever the hell he is at the moment."

Neil actually winced. "In here you are totally private. There are no cameras in the flat, but out in the hall there are. So if you were to leave, I'll know it. I'm in another flat across the way. Not far. Mr. Blackstone really just wants you to make yourself at home." He put his phone up to his ear and jogged it. "Call me if you need anything, Brynne."

The door latch clicked and my protector was gone.

Well, this was weird. Alone in Ethan's home with my overnight bag and a scrambled head. I wondered if I would ever feel normal again.

First things first, I went to the fridge, took out a chilled water bottle and drained half of it. The inside of Ethan's refrigerator was well stocked with plenty of fresh things to work with, so no problem on the dinner. I explored his coffeemaker next and started drooling. *Very nice indeed.* I set a pot to brewing and checked out his Sub-Zero freezer. Ethan's housekeeper appeared organized to the point of labeled and dated frozen meals in nice plastic containers for easy identification. I passed on those. I wasn't really hungry anyway after the massive Chinese lunch he'd fed me at his office.

I moved on to the bedroom and was instantly hit with remembrances of the last time I was in this room. I closed my eyes and breathed in the scent of Ethan. He was everywhere even when he wasn't. I stepped into his bathroom. The grotto shower of travertine marble was gorgeous, but that magnificent tub was a fantasy for a girl who did not have a proper bathtub in her flat. I knew what I was going to do first.

An hour later my skin was pink from the heat and soft from the bubbles. I'd dressed in my Jimi Hendrix T-shirt and a pair of Ethan's silk boxers that were very swishy on me. I'd organized my purchases from Boots in a bathroom drawer, shaved my legs and slathered myself in primrose-scented lotion.

I wandered back to the coffeemaker and fixed myself a mug before drifting into the other rooms of Ethan's flat. The home gym had a state-of-the-art treadmill facing the floor-to-ceiling windows. The view took my breath away. I love a city lights view, but I imagined it was just as spectacular in the daytime.

I found what I believed to be his office and turned the handle. The room behind the door was indeed an office. A massive oak desk anchored the room while the opposing wall held a panel of TV monitors and other high-tech equipment. But it was the wall behind the desk that really caught my attention: a saltwater aquarium glowed with light and colors and bubbles over the rippling water. I came closer and took in the rainbow of fish darting around elegant coral formations. The lionfish did not dart. He came up to the glass and fluttered an array of multicolored fins at me as if in greeting.

"Hey, handsome. What does he call you, I wonder?" I spoke to my fishy companion and sipped my coffee.

I ate a cherry yogurt at the kitchen bar and fixed a second cup of coffee. One whole wall of the main room held shelves of books. I perused his collection, which was eclectic to say the least. Classics, mysteries, mainstream stuff and tons of historical fiction filled out most of it. There was some military history and books on photography. A large amount on statistics and gambling too. He had popular fiction and even a few books of poetry, which made me smile. I liked that Ethan valued books.

I snagged a book of letters Keats had written to Fanny Brawne and took it into the living room to sit on the sofa and enjoy. I had my coffee, angsty love letters from a poet to his girl and the twinkling night lights of London displayed before me.

I spent a nice hour before I set the book aside. I looked out at the city. This was the spot where Ethan had undressed me, right in front of his balcony window. He'd stepped back and told me that nothing compared to the sight of me standing in his house. *Oh, Ethan.*

I decided to text him: **Brynne Bennett: <--- is pissed at u about the Neil thing. R u crazy?!!!**

It didn't take him but a moment to get back to me: **Ethan Blackstone: <--- crazy for u & we need to talk about things. Miss u very much.**

Understatement of the year! **Brynne Bennett: <--- is wearing ur boxers right now and u better believe it, buster!**

I had to laugh at the next part: **Ethan Blackstone: <--- just got a hard-on picturing u in my shorts. Pls leave on pillow cuz I'm never laundering.**

Brynne Bennett: <--- still pissed and thinks u have a beautiful coffeemaker.

Ethan Blackstone: <--- thinks I have a beautiful girlfriend. Did u eat sthg?

Brynne Bennett: <--- ate sthg. U have a pet lionfish. :)

That is Simba. I pamper him & he tolerates me. U 2 have much in common. His response made me smile. Ethan had a soft spot for animals, apparently.

I fired back: **Ur getting no more BJ's just 4 that comment. :P**

Ethan Blackstone: <--- so wants to spank u right now & kiss u & shag u. Ur killing me baby!!

Brynne Bennett: <--- is getting sleepy. Gonna take pill and get in ur bed. Don't tease me.

Never! Go 2 sleep my beauty. I will find u.

I got up from Ethan's sofa and headed back to the kitchen to wash up. I cleaned out the coffeemaker and set it up for the morning. All I would have to do is start it. I used my new purple toothbrush and took the pill. The supersoft sheets of Ethan's bed smelled of him; soothing and comforting me in my solitude. I filled my head with his scent and crashed.

Firm arms held me. The smell I adored floated around me. Lips kissed me. I opened my eyes to the night and saw shadows. I knew who was with me, though. My waking was peaceful and gentle, something good, and for me, a totally new experience.

"You're here," I murmured against his lips.

"And so are you," he whispered. "I fucking love finding you in my bed."

Ethan's hands had been busy in my sleep. I was naked from the waist down, his silk boxers long removed. Ethan was naked too. I could feel his hard muscles and solid flesh trying to meld with mine. My shirt was pushed up and my breasts were being devoured by his rasping lips, whiskers tickling the sensitive flesh, teasing my nipples with sucking pulls until I was a moaning, writhing creature beneath him.

I buried my hands in his hair and felt the movement of his head as he worshipped my nipples and plumped the weight of my breasts with his hand. He stopped and pulled my shirt all the way off and stared down at me, hungry and beautiful. The light from the master bath filtered in enough to allow me some vision of him, and I was glad. I need to see Ethan when he comes to me. It reassures me that I will be safe with him.

"Your bed smells like you," I said.

"You are the only thing I want to smell, and right now I need the taste of you in my mouth." Then he spread me wide and descended.

"Oh, God, Ethan!" The work of his tongue on my cleft,

swirling and smoothing over heated flesh opened to him, switched me from sleepy to sexed in less than a second. I couldn't keep still even though he held me down and open at the inner thighs. The orgasm came upon me so fast and so violently that I heard myself shout through it, riding his tongue like a wanton, my muscles clenching and throbbing in scorching pleasure.

Ethan growled against my pussy lips and pulled away, probably staring at what he wanted to take with his cock. He didn't ask. Ethan took.

He lifted my legs over his shoulders and pierced me hard and deep. He made sounds as his cock filled me. I was pinned by his invasion while still reeling with an orgasm, so I could only hang on as he fucked me. The sex was fiery and demanding with him telling me how good I felt and how much he wanted me here in his bed and how beautiful I was. All words to bring me closer to him. More dependent on him. More tangled up in his world. I knew it.

Ethan made me climax again; nearly punishing strokes meant to claim first and pleasure secondly. But the pleasure was exquisite when it arrived simultaneous with him filling me up with his own explosive orgasm. I felt tears sliding down to the sheets as I accepted what he gave to me. He choked out my name, his eyes locked onto mine like the other times. I knew he saw my tears.

He moved my legs off his shoulders and propped himself against me, holding my face and stroking, his blue eyes searching, still buried in me flexing slow and deep with his talented cock, drawing out the pleasure. "You're mine," he whispered.

"I know," I whispered back to him. Ethan kissed me reverently with our bodies joined; gentle explorations of my lips and feathery pulls and nibbles with teeth that only grazed. He held on to me and kissed me for a long time before he finally moved out of my body.

Fucking Ethan can only be described as beautiful in my head. I know to others it would be pornographic, but to me it was simply a beautiful act of us together. To be intimate like that with him wanting me so intensely was an addictive drug. More potent than anything I'd ever experienced before in my life. I think I could forgive Ethan just about anything that he might do to hurt me. And this was my very great mistake.

Chapter 11

Ethan brought me my coffee in bed the next morning. I sat up against the headboard and pulled the sheet up to cover myself. He raised an eyebrow as he sat down on the edge of the bed and carefully handed the mug over. "I think I did it right, but you have a taste and tell me."

I took a sip and made a face.

"I put half cream and three spoonfuls of sugar," he said with a shrug. "You set up the coffee yourself. All I did was press brew on the machine."

I kept him hanging for another minute before cracking a smile and taking another sip of my delicious coffee.

"What? Just making sure you're trained in proper coffee prep. I have my standards." I winked at him. "I think you'll do in a pinch, Mr. Blackstone."

"You devil woman, teasing me like that." He leaned in to kiss me, careful of the hot coffee. "I like having the coffeemaker set up the night before. I wonder why I never thought of it." He stayed close to my face, looking intently over me, his hair still messy from sleep and all the sex and still managing to look like a god. "I think you should be here every night to set it up just before you get in my bed." He put his mouth right at my neck and grazed. "So I can bring you your coffee like this in the mornings, with you all naked and lovely, and the smell of me all over you from a night of shagging."

I shivered from the words and the images of that reality, but we still had things to discuss. And this was an issue between Ethan and me. We didn't talk enough about what needed to be worked through. When he got near me, the clothing dropped away, my body responded to him, and well, not much talking ever got done after that.

"Ethan," I said gently, my hand at his cheek to stop him, "we need to talk about what's going on. The bodyguard thing with Neil? Why would you do that and not tell me?"

"I was going to tell you last night after I brought you here but it didn't work out like that." His face fell away from me and he looked down. "The city is full of strangers right now, baby. You are a beautiful woman and I don't think it's safe for you to be taking the Tube and walking all over on your own. Remember that fucking idiot at the club."

"But I was doing that before I met you, and I was just fine."

"I know you were. And you were not my girlfriend then either." He gave me one of his Ethan looks—the kind where I tense up and wait for the blast of Arctic air to hit me. "I run a security firm, Brynne. It's what I do. How can I have you going all over London when I know the dangers?" He put a hand up to my face and started in with the thumb-rubbing action. "Please? For me?" He put his forehead against mine. "If something happened to you it would kill me."

I brought one hand up to his hair and dug my fingers in. "Oh, Ethan, you want a great deal from me, and sometimes I just feel like I'm getting pulled under. There's so much about me that you don't know." He started to speak and I shushed him with my fingers over his mouth. "Things I am not ready to share just yet. You said we could go slow."

He kissed my fingers pressed to his lips and then tugged them down. "I know, baby. I did. And I don't want to do anything to jeopardize you and me." He kissed my neck and nipped at my earlobe. "Can we talk about a compromise?" he whispered.

I tugged at his hair so he would stop the seduction tactics and look at me. "First you need to actually talk to me and not try to distract me with sex. You're very good at distracting me, Ethan. Just tell me what you want me to do and I'll tell you if I can do it."

"How about you accept a driver?" He took a finger and traced over the tops of my breasts where the sheet was slipping down. "No more walks to the Tube and hailing cabs in the dark. You have a car to take you anywhere you want to go"—he paused and pinned me with his very expressive eyes that told me so much about his desire to protect me—"and I can have some peace of mind."

I took another sip of the coffee he'd brought to me and decided to ask my own pointed question. "And why do you need peace of mind about me?"

"Because you're very special, Brynne."

"How special, Ethan?" I whispered, because I was a little frightened to hear it. I was frightened of my own feelings for him already. In such a short time he'd possessed me.

"For me? As special as it gets, baby." He smiled his signature one-side-up twist and made my stomach flutter.

He didn't say he loved me. But I hadn't said it to him either. I knew he cared about me, though.

He looked down again and picked up my free hand palm up. My wrist scar showed. The one I'm ashamed of and try to hide, but is impossible to conceal when it's daylight and I am naked. He traced over the jagged line with his fingertip, so gentle it felt like a caress. He did not ask me how I got my scar and I did not offer to tell him. The pain of remembering added to the shame, paralyzed me from talking about it.

I had feelings for this man but I couldn't share that with him quite yet. My indignity was too ugly and horrid to bring between us. Right now I just wanted to be wanted. Ethan wanted me. And that was enough to make me agree. Baby steps. I would accept his conditions for a driver, and he would accept my inability to share my past with him. We would go slow.

"Okay." I leaned forward and kissed him on the throat above the vee of his T-shirt, the hairs of his chest tickling my mouth, his male scent already familiar to the point of downright necessity along with food and water and breathing. "I'll accept the driver and you'll tell me up front what you're doing. I need honesty. I like that you are so blunt with me. You tell me what you want and I get it—"

"Thank you." He started kissing me again. My coffee was set aside and the sheet was tugged away. Ethan pulled his shirt off and ditched the sweatpants and stretched out over me. I finally got a really good look at his body. Completely naked. In the light.

Sweet Jesus!

From his chiseled chest and tight nipples down to his impressive and beautiful cock, I was mesmerized. He was trimmed up neatly, nothing weird, just nice and totally masculine.

He stopped and tilted his head. "What?"

I pushed him back so he sat on his knees, and pulled my own self up. "I want to look at you." I trailed my hands over him, over his nipples and that V-cut so sinfully sculpted it was truly unfair to the rest of the male population, to his thighs hard with muscles and dusted with dark hair. He let me touch him and control the moment. "You're beautiful, Ethan."

He made a sound in his throat and his body shuddered. Our eyes met and there was an exchange; a communication of feelings and an understanding of where we were heading in this force connecting us.

I looked down at his shaft, hard and pulsing. A drop at the tip confirmed how ready he was for me. I wanted him so badly I hurt. I wanted to give him pleasure and make him come apart like he had me, totally blown into a million fragments. I lowered my head and took his beautiful penis into my mouth. I got my wish a few minutes later.

We broke in the shower too, or I should say I did when he propped me in the corner, dropped to his knees and returned the favor. The sex never ended with this man. And I was on board the sexy train right with him, flashing my frequent traveler pass. I had not had so much sex in—

Don't go there and don't ruin this time with him.

Ethan had a tattoo on his back. Right across his shoulders and even extending over his deltoids were medium-sized horizontal wings. They looked a little Goth and almost Greco-Roman in their black inked starkness. I loved the quote underneath the wings. *No more yielding but a dream.* I saw it in the shower when he turned to get the soap.

"That's Shakespeare, right?" I smoothed over the ink with my hand, and that's when I saw the scars. Many white lines and ridges. So many you couldn't count them. I gasped a sharp breath, desperately sad to think about how badly he'd been hurt. I wanted to ask, but I held my tongue. I didn't offer to tell about my scars.

He turned back around and kissed me on the lips before I could say another word. Ethan didn't want to talk about his scars any more than I wanted to talk about mine.

More than a week of nights at Ethan's place and I needed to get back to my flat for other than a grab of fresh clothing. I needed a recharge in my own home. Ethan agreed to come over here tonight. I told him slumming was good for the soul. He teased me back, saying it wouldn't matter as long as we had something to eat and a bed because we'd both be naked for his sleepover. I told him that if Gaby showed up he'd have to get dressed; that I wasn't going to allow my roommate the chance to lust after my boyfriend's godlike physique. He laughed and told me he loved the sound of jealousy in my voice. I told him to show up hungry for dinner and fully clothed. He was still laughing when we hung up.

I changed into some yoga pants and a soft T-shirt after Neil dropped me back home. He'd picked me up from the Rothvale, plus a quick stop at the supermarket for ingredients for the Mexican dinner I'd planned. Ethan knew that Mexican food was my favorite, and I was determined to recruit him to my team. On the menu tonight? Chicken tacos with corn salsa and avocado. If Ethan hated it, then I would fix him a burrito. No guy can resist a burrito packed with meat, beans, cheese and guacamole. I hope. Brits were weird about food.

As soon as I got the chicken started and my hands were washed I decided to call my dad. It would be morning for him but he'd be at work by now, and if he wasn't too busy we could have a chat. I set my phone on speaker and dialed his office.

"Tom Bennett."

"Hey, Daddy."

"Princess! I've missed hearing your sweet voice. This is a surprise." I smiled at my dad's choice of name for me. He'd been calling me Princess ever since I could remember. And now that I was nearly twenty-five years old, he didn't seem bothered in the slightest about continuing with the nickname either.

"I thought I'd call you for a change. I just miss you."

"Is everything all right over there in London? Getting excited for the Olympics? How was Benny's show? Did you like how your pictures looked when they were blown up huge on canvas?"

I laughed. "That was four questions all at once, Dad. Give a girl a break, would ya!"

"Sorry, Princess, I just get excited to hear from you. You're so far away and busy with your life. The proofs you sent of your photos were magnificent. Tell me about Benny's show."

"Well, it was a success. Ben did well and the pictures sold. I've had some more jobs too, so I'm just taking it slow and we'll see where this leads." I was happy I could talk to my dad like this and that he supported my modeling. He thought it was good for me, unlike my mother, who was embarrassed by her daughter posing sans clothing.

"You're going to be famous the world over," he said. "I'm proud of you, Princess. I think that the modeling is going to help you. I hope you feel that way." He sounded a little off to me, almost sad. "What are you doing right now?"

"I'm making dinner. Tacos. I have a friend coming over in a bit. Dad, is everything okay with you?"

He hesitated for a moment before answering me. I could tell there was something on his mind. "Brynnie, you heard about the plane that went down and Congressman Woodson's death?"

"Yeah. He was the one they were going to tap for vice president? That was big news even for over here. Why, Dad?"

"Have you heard about who is replacing Woodson on the ticket?"

I never expected the name he told me. And just like that the past reared up and dug its claws in again.

"Oh no! Do *not* tell me Senator Oakley got the nomination! You've got to be kidding me if that—that—*man* could be the next vice president of the United States! How is it possible they want him? Daddy—"

"I know, sweetheart. He's been working his way up the food chain these last years. First state senator and now U.S. senator—"

"Yeah, well, I hope they all go down in a big ball of flames."

"Brynnie, this is serious stuff. There'll be digging into his past to find dirt on Oakley—on his family—by the incumbent party. I want you to be careful. If anyone approaches you or sends you anything suspicious, you need to let me know right away. These people have the resources to dig down deep. They are like sharks. When they scent even a drop of blood, get ready for a sneak attack."

"Well, Senator Oakley is the guy with the demon seed for a son. I'd say he has a very *big* problem then."

"I know, sweetie. And Oakley's people will work just as hard to keep his family secrets buried. It's not a nice situation, and I hate that you're so far away from home. But I do think in this case it might be a good thing that you're in London. I don't want anyone to hurt you, and the further removed you are the better. No evil stories to surface in the news or . . . anything else."

Like a video. I knew that's what my dad was thinking of. That video was still out floating around in cyberspace somewhere.

"You're doing so well, Princess. I can hear it in your voice, and that makes your old dad smile. So who is this friend you're cooking dinner for? It's not a man, is it?"

I smiled as I mixed up the corn salsa. "Well, I met someone, Dad. He's really special in a lot of ways. He bought my picture at Benny's show. That's how we met."

"Really."

"Yeah." It felt weird telling my dad about Ethan all of a sudden. Maybe because I'd never talked to him about boyfriends much. There had never been reason to. I hadn't wanted one for a long, long time.

"Tell me more. What does he do for a living? How old is he? Oh, and go ahead and let me have his number while you're at it. I need to give him a call and set him straight on the ground rules with my baby girl."

I laughed nervously. "Well, I think it's a little late for that, Dad. Ethan's pretty special, like I said. We spend a lot of time together. He really listens to me and I feel truly . . . happy with him. He understands me."

Dad got quiet for a minute. I think he was shocked to hear me talk about a man like I really cared. And I shouldn't have been too surprised either. Ethan was the first in a long line of *firsts* with me.

"What is this Ethan's last name and what does he do for a living?"

"Blackstone. He's thirty-two and he owns a private security company. He's so paranoid he has me assigned to a driver so I won't take the Tube to get around. All the influx of people for the Olympics has him nervous. So you don't have to worry about my safety at all. Ethan is a pro."

"Wow, that does sound serious. Are you . . . are you guys sleep—in a relationship?"

I laughed again, this time feeling sorry for my dad in his obvious discomfort. "Yeah, Dad. We're having a relationship. I told you, this one's special." I waited into the silence on the other end of the phone and started warming tortillas. "In fact he won some big poker tournaments in the States about six years ago. I thought you might have heard of him."

"Hmmmm," Dad muttered. "Maybe, I'd have to check." I heard some muffled talking in the background.

"I should let you go, Dad. You're working, and I just wanted to say hi and tell you what's been happening with me. I'm doing well and things are good."

"Okay, Princess. I'm so glad you called. And I'm happy if my baby girl is happy. Be safe and tell your new boyfriend if he hurts you he is a *dead* boyfriend. Don't forget. And give him my number too. Tell him your dad wants to have a little man-to-man with him sometime. We can talk about poker."

I laughed. "Right. Will do, Daddy. Love you!"

Ethan walked in just as I ended the call. He had a six-pack of Dos Equis and a predatory smile on his face. I'd given my key to Neil, who passed it along to Ethan so he could get in downstairs. He plunked down my key and the beer on the counter before asking, "Did I hear you telling someone you loved them just as I came in?"

I grinned and nodded slowly. "It was a man too."

He came up behind me at the counter, put his hands to my shoulders and started rubbing. I leaned into his hard body and let myself enjoy the massage. "That bloke is one lucky fellow then. Wonder what he did that was so special." He peeked down at the food sorted out in bowls and snagged a piece of cooked chicken. "Mmmmm," he said as he savored it, his mouth at my neck.

"Well, he read me bedtime stories. Combed out my wet hair without snagging and hurting. Taught me how to ride a bike and how to swim. He always kissed my boo-boos when I got scraped, and most importantly, opened his wallet frequently, but that wasn't until later."

Ethan grunted, "I can do all those things for you and more." He stole another piece of chicken. "Especially the *more* part."

I smacked his hand away. "Thief!"

"You're a good cook," he murmured against my ear. "I think I must keep you."

"So you do like my Mexican dinner. I see you went with the theme and brought us Dos Equis. Smart move, Blackstone. You've got potential." I started moving bowls to the table.

"Dos Equis is from Mexico?" He made a noise and shrugged. "I just chose that one because I like the ads . . . The Most Interesting Man in the World." He grinned malevolently and helped me transfer the rest of the food.

"A liar and a thief." I shook my head sadly. "You just blew all your potential, Blackstone."

"I'll change your mind later I'm sure, Bennett." He grinned over at me from the sink, where he washed his hands quickly and then opened two beers for us. "I have an abundance of *potential*," he said, wiggling his eyebrows. Ethan delivered my Dos Equis and looked over everything set out on the table, head tilted in perusal. "Help me out here. How do I put your chicken tacos together? They smell very nice, by the way."

I couldn't help laughing at him. The way he said "tacos" in his British accent cracked me up. And how he worded things too. It just made me laugh.

"What's so funny? Am I amusing you now, Miss Bennett?"

"Here, let me fix it." I showed him how to put some

chicken, corn salsa, a dollop of sour cream, a sprinkle of shredded cheese and a couple slices of avocado on the tortilla and fold it. "You're just adorable, that's all, Mr. Blackstone. That accent of yours—it makes me laugh sometimes." I handed him his taco on the plate.

"Ahhh, so I went from losing all my potential to adorable in a very short time. And just by speaking." He accepted the plate and waited for me to fix mine. "I'll have to remember that, baby." He flashed one of those million-dollar Ethan smiles at me and took a sip of his beer.

"So go ahead and take a bite. Give me your verdict and be aware that I will *know* if you lie to me." I tapped my head. "Super powers of deduction." I picked up my taco and took a bite, moaning in overexaggerated sounds of pleasure and arching my neck back. "So delicious I feel hot all over," I purred across the table.

Ethan looked at me like I'd just sprouted devil horns and swallowed hard in his throat. I knew he would get me back later for the merciless teasing. I didn't care. Ethan was fun. We had fun together, and that was part of what I loved about him. *Love.* Did I love him?

He lifted the taco to his mouth and took a bite. He stared at me as he chewed and swallowed. He wiped his mouth on a napkin and looked up in contemplation, pretending to count on his fingers. He took another sip of beer.

"Well, let's see." He focused on me. "Chef Bennett, I give you a five on execution. Laughing at me got you a five-point deduction right out the gate. I think a six on presentation—all that moaning and thrusting at the dinner table was a bit unfair, don't you think? And a nine-point-five on taste." He took another bite and grinned. "How did I do?"

He was so handsome sitting there at my table, eating the tacos I'd made, and sweetly telling me he liked my cooking, and just being Ethan, that I knew the answer to my question all in an instant. Did I love Ethan? *Yes. I do love him.*

Chapter 12

Surprising Ethan at his office seemed like a good idea, but I wasn't willing to do it without some assistance. I enlisted Elaina's help first. I really liked her. She seemed honest and very straightforward, which I respected in a person. She was also engaged to Neil. I found that out after I started sleeping over at Ethan's place. One morning when we hit the elevators to leave for work, I saw Elaina and Neil coming out of the flat on the other wing, hand in hand. Ethan saw my surprise and told me they were getting married in the fall.

I was relieved Elaina didn't act jealous about her

fiancé driving me around London. I think she was happy that Ethan had a girlfriend. I'd noticed that his employees really seemed to care about him. And I liked that too.

"Hi, Elaina, it's Brynne."

"Hello, Brynne. Why didn't you call through to his mobile?" Smart girl, Elaina, always aware of logistics.

"I was thinking of surprising him with lunch. Can you check his schedule for me?"

I heard some flipping of pages and then she put me on hold. "He is in office today. Busy with conference calls and such, but no appointments away on his schedule."

"Thanks, Elaina. I would just ask Frances, but Ethan has her on speaker and he hears when I call so I can't do a surprise. Can I bring you all something from King's Delicatessen? I am just going to pick up sandwiches, but I was thinking if you could get Frances to tell Ethan she was ordering, then he won't know it's me being lunch lady today."

Elaina laughed and put me on hold again while she got food orders from everyone. "Frances told me to tell you she likes your style, Brynne. Keeping the boss on his toes is good for him."

"I think so too," I said, writing down the sandwich orders. "Thanks for your help, and I should be there within the hour."

We hung up and I phoned the delicatessen to order the food, and then Neil for a ride. I cleared up my area and organized supplies while I waited. I was done here for the day and wouldn't be returning for nearly a week. Final exams were coming and I needed to study. My plan was to hole up at Ethan's place and hit the books while he worked, use his home gym and magnificent coffeemaker, and basically go off the radar for a while. I needed the time, and so did my grades.

I took a last look at *Lady Percival* and felt a burst of pride. She had come along nicely, and the best part was I now knew the name of the book she held in her hands. Ethan had helped me solve the mystery when he'd brought me to work one morning and I'd invited him back here.

The book my mysterious lady held was in fact so special and so rare that the Mallerton Society wanted her included in the exhibition even though she was not even close to being fully conserved. They wanted to showcase her as an example of how ambiguous clues can be revealed with proper restoration and cleaning. The disclosure of what she held in her hand had also enhanced the provenance for the artist in general. Sir Tristan Mallerton was now enjoying a renaissance of renewed interest and exposure even though he'd been dead for a very long time.

My phone buzzed with a text from Neil. He'd arrived outside, so I gathered my things and took off, waving to Rory as I checked out.

Neil helped me with the food and used a company credit card to pay for everything, which got him a stern look from me.

"Well, he thinks Frances ordered lunch, and this is how he does it. If you pay he'll be a right prick about it when he finds out," Neil said.

"Has he always been so controlling, Neil?" I asked once we were back in the car and on our way. Neil and I had developed an easy rapport. We respected the other's position and needs, so the relationship worked.

"No." Neil shook his head. "E had a hard edge to him when he got out of the SF. But then war changes everybody who gets too close to it. E got as close as it gets and made it out alive. He's a walking miracle."

"I've seen his scars," I said.

"Did he tell you about what happened in Afghanistan?" Neil looked up at me in the rearview.

"No," I answered truthfully, realizing that the information coming from Neil would stop and I would be no closer to understanding Ethan's past than he would be about knowing mine.

Elaina helped us dole out the food to the proper parties and Frances ushered me into Ethan's inner sanctum with a smug look and shut the door. He was on the phone.

My gorgeous guy was busy with work but still held out his hand to me. I set the sandwiches on his desk and went to him. He snaked his arm around me and pulled me down onto his lap, and kept right on with his business call.

"Right, I know. But you tell those fools that Blackstone represents the Royal Family, and when Her Majesty shows up for the opening ceremonies to give her blessing there will not be one fucking exit left unattended. Period. No negotiation."

Ethan continued with his call and I began unpacking his lunch. He moved his hand up to the back of my neck and rubbed. It felt divine with him touching me even though any idiot could see he was dreadfully busy.

I set out his food on a plate and then unwrapped mine. I bit into my chicken salad on wheat while he massaged my neck. A girl could seriously get used to this. Ethan was so affectionate, and I loved the way he wanted to touch me all the time. My touchy-feely guy. I was nearly done with half of my sandwich before he ended his call.

Both hands reached and turned me, still on his lap. He gave me a very nice kiss and groaned. "Finally. It's like talking to a brick wall sometimes," he muttered. He smiled at me and looked at the plate. "You brought me lunch . . . and your delicious self."

I smiled back. "I did."

"Which should I devour first, the sandwich or you?" He wiggled his eyebrows at me, his hands starting to roam up the side of my sweater.

"I think you better devour your sandwich before you get another phone call," I told him.

His phone rang.

He scowled and resigned himself to it. The second call was relatively quick, though, and he managed to start his roast beef on rye before the third one came through. He put that call on speaker so he could eat and converse at the same time. Not very elegant, but it worked.

I was content to sit with him and listen to his work business while he smoothed a hand up and down my back. Ethan made me feel glad I had stopped by even though this would be no social lunch for us. The timing was crazy for him and me. I couldn't imagine his job could be any more complicated than at the moment with the Olympics looming and London hosting the whole thing. He should have just sent me a note that said, "I just bought your portrait and I'd really like to get to know you—sometime in mid-August."

He kept his phone on speaker and we managed a few quick kisses in between calls and bites, but soon it was hard to justify as a lunch hour anymore.

"I should get going, Ethan." I kissed him and started to get up.

"No." He held me on his lap. "I don't want you to go yet. I like having you here with me. You soothe me, baby." He rested his head on top of mine. "You are my ray of light in a fog of ignorance and frustration."

"Really? You like that I came and complicated your day and forced food on you?" I fiddled with his tie clip and smoothed his tie. "You're so busy with your work, and I'm interrupting."

"No, you're not," he traced his lips along my throat. "It tells me that you care for me," he said quietly.

"I do, Ethan," I whispered back.

"So you'll stay for a while?"

How could I say no to him when he was so sweet with me? "All right, just an hour more. But then I have to really go. I need to stop by my flat and get some things. I have to study for exams, and I want to get in a workout. You're not the only one around here that's busy." I tweaked his chin and made him grin at me.

"I want to get busy with you right here on my desk," he growled and lifted me up, plopping me ass first on his big executive desk.

I squeaked as he pounced, pushing my legs apart so he could get in between with his hips. "Ethan! Your office! We can't!"

He reached under his desk, and I heard the click of the door locking. "I want you so badly right now. I need you, Brynne. Please?"

He was all over me, hands gripping, pushing me back on the desk and thrusting hard at my center. I let him press me down and slide me to the edge, my body already softening and heating up for him. His purposeful long fingers made their way to my panties and peeled those babies right down my legs, over my boots and dropped somewhere on the floor of his office. I'd found that Ethan was definitely an opportunist whenever I chose to wear a skirt.

"You're a crazy man," I murmured, not really caring anymore that we were about to fuck on his desk in the middle of his place of work.

"Crazy for you," he said, fingering my clit and getting me wet. I heard his belt jingle and then his zipper go down. And then he was sinking that delicious heat all the way in me, slow and deep.

He leaned over me and took my face in both hands. He kissed me hard, thrusting his tongue into my mouth as he liked to do. Ethan dominated during sex. He wanted his tongue and his fingers and his cock in me all at once. Like that way he could claim me more completely. I don't know why, it was just his way. And I loved it. His way was honest and totally direct. I knew what I would get with Ethan, and it always ended with an orgasm that left me trembling.

Ethan started moving and so did I. We were wild with it too. Totally abandoned and lustfully fucking on top of his desk when the phone rang. He'd left it on speaker. "Don't answer it," I gasped, nearly ready to climax.

"Hell, no," he grunted, pounding faster into me, his cock swelling to the bone-hard density it got right before he came.

He slid his magic fingers over my clit and I broke apart, biting down on my lip to keep from crying out. Ethan was not far behind me. He covered my mouth with his to keep us both from shouting and pumped his orgasm inside me.

The unanswered call went to voice mail, but still on speaker.

"Ethan Blackstone is unavailable. Please leave your message and number where you can be reached."

The beep sounded and we panted at each other, our faces just inches apart. I smiled at him. He smoothed my hair so gently and kissed me like a lover would. I felt precious to him. He made me feel that way.

"You're an asshole, Blackstone. I hired you to protect my daughter, not to fuck her! She's been through hell, and the last thing she needs is another heartbreaking betrayal. The way she talks I think she's in love with you—"

Ethan fumbled with the phone to shut it down, but it was too late. I heard my father's voice on the phone. I knew . . . the truth about Ethan and me. I shoved at him, fighting to get him off.

"Brynne, no! Please let me explain—"

He looked white as a sheet and totally stone-cold terrified as he held me under him, our bodies still joined.

"Get off me. Get your cock out of me and let me go, you motherfucking liar!"

He held me to him, eyes on me. "Baby . . . listen to me. I was going to tell you—I was ready to a long time ago, but I didn't want to bring up bad memories for you. I don't want to hurt you—"

"Get. Off. Me. Now."

"Please don't leave. Brynne, I—I—didn't mean to hurt you, but I was protecting you from remembering. There's a threat out there to your safety ... and then I met you ... and I couldn't stop wanting you. I couldn't stay away from you." He tried to kiss me.

I turned my face away and closed my eyes. All the trust I had for this man was gone. In its place a terrible ache filled my heart. He knew about me. He knew what had happened to me. Probably had seen the video. And now there were people out to hurt me? Why? He was hired by my dad and all this time he knew and I didn't. How could he? How could he be the Ethan I'd fallen in love with and betray me like this?

"Waterloo." I turned back and stared.

"No ... no ... no," he chanted. "Please no, Brynne." He shook his head back and forth, his eyes devastated.

"Water-fucking-loo, Ethan. And if you don't get off me I will scream the walls down." I spoke clear and soft, my heart hardened and bleeding black blood. *Blackstone blood.*

He moved out of me and helped me sit up. I hopped off his desk and lunged for my bag. He zipped up his pants and tried again. "Brynne, baby, I—I love you. I love you so much; I would do anything not to hurt you. I'm sorry, I'm sorry, I'm so fucking sorry."

I tried to get out the door, but it wouldn't budge. "Unlock it," I demanded.

"Did you hear me just now?"

I looked at him and nodded. "Open the door so I can leave." I spoke very evenly, surprised I was not a weeping wreck crumpled to the floor. I just needed to get out of here and to my flat. I had one purpose, and it was to flee to safety.

He rubbed his head and looked down, then moved to his desk and reached the button or whatever it was that held me in. I heard the click and I was out of there.

"Thank you for the delicious lunch, dear," Frances called as I bailed.

I waved at her but was unable to speak. I just walked out. I had my purse and no underwear, but I wasn't going back in there to find them. *Just get me out of here and home . . . just get me out of here and home . . . just get me out—*

Oh my God, I was leaving Ethan. We were done. He'd lied to me and I couldn't trust him anymore. He said he loved me. Is that what lovers do? They lie?

I didn't speak to Elaina at reception either when I headed for the elevators. I pushed the call button and realized he was right behind me. Ethan had chased me down and still I didn't break.

"Brynne . . . baby, please don't leave like this. God, I—I fucked up. I love you. Please—"

He put his hand on my shoulder and I flinched. "No you don't," was all I could manage.

"Yes I do!" he yelled, his voice getting angry. "You can leave me, but I'll still be protecting you. I'll still be watching over you to make sure you're safe and that nobody can hurt you!"

"What about you hurting me?" I spat back at him. "And you're fired, Ethan. Don't ever contact me again." The elevator dinged and the doors opened. I stepped in and turned around to face him.

He rolled his head up and opened his mouth in a pleading gesture that told me he was hurting. Not as bad as I was, but he looked ragged and desperate. "Brynne . . . don't do this," he begged as the doors started to close me in alone.

I heard a loud bang coupled with one very comprehensible f-bomb shouted as the car started to take me down. Down to the street where I would hail a cab to drive me home to my flat. Where I would fall apart as soon as I could get inside, and where I would crawl into my bed and curl up and try to forget him. Ethan Blackstone. I was doomed to failure. I knew that. I would never be able to forget Ethan. Never.

About the Author

Raine has been reading romance novels since she picked up that first Barbara Cartland paperback at the tender age of thirteen. She thinks it was *The Flame Is Love* from 1975. And it's a safe bet she'll never stop reading romance novels because now she writes them too. Granted, Raine's stories are edgy enough to turn Ms. Cartland in her grave, but to her way of thinking, a tall, dark and handsome hero never goes out of fashion. Never! Writing sexy romance stories pretty much fills her days now. Raine has a prince of a husband and two brilliant sons to pull her back into the real world if the writing takes her too far away. Her sons know she likes to write stories but have never asked to read any. (Raine is so very grateful about this.) She loves to hear from readers and chat about the characters in her books. You can connect with Raine on Facebook or visit her blog at RaineMiller.com to see what she's working on now.

If you enjoyed this book, then you will be happy to know that Part 2 is on its way. I made the decision, as a fun insight into the male mind, to write the next part from Ethan's point of view. Please have a first look at Chapter 1 of *All In*, The Blackstone Affair, Part 2, where the story of Brynne and Ethan continues with lots of passion, surprises, and, of course, love.

SNEAK PEEK

All In

THE BLACKSTONE AFFAIR
BOOK 2

Chapter 1

My hand throbbed along with my heartbeat. All I could do was breathe at the now sealed doors of the lift that was taking her away from me.

Think for one moment!

Chasing after her was not an option, so I left the lobby and went into the break room. Elaina was in getting coffee. She kept her head down and pretended I wasn't there. Smart woman. I hope those idiots on the floor do the same or they just might need to find new jobs.

I threw some ice into a plastic bag and shoved my hand inside. Fuck, it stung! There was blood on my knuckles and I'm certain on the wall next to the lift. I walked back out to my office with my hand in the ice. I told Frances to call maintenance to come and fix the bloody ding in the wall.

Frances nodded without missing a beat and looked at the bag of ice at the end of my arm. "Do you need an X-ray for that?" she asked, her expression like that of a mum. What I envisioned a mother would look like, at least. I barely remember mine, so I'm probably merely projecting with her.

"No." *I need my girl back, not some fucking X-ray!*

I went through to my office and shut myself in. I pulled out a bottle of Van Gogh from the bar fridge and cracked it. Opening my desk drawer, I fumbled for the pack of Djarum Blacks and the lighter I liked to keep in there. I'd been plowing through the smokes at a record pace since meeting Brynne. I'd have to remember to stock up.

Now all I needed was a glass for the vodka, or maybe not. The bottle would do me just fine. I took a swig with my busted hand and welcomed the pain.

Fuck my hand; it's my heart that's broken.

I stared at her picture. The one I took of her at work when she showed me the painting of Lady Percival with the book. I remembered how I'd used my mobile to take the photo and was pleasantly surprised to see how nice it came out. So nice, in fact, I downloaded it and ordered a print for my office. Didn't matter it was only the camera in a mobile phone—Brynne looked beautiful through any lens. Especially the lenses of my eyes. Sometimes it almost hurt to look at her.

I recalled that morning with her. I could just see her in my mind's eye—how happy she was when I snapped the photo of her smiling down at that old painting . . .

I had parked in the lot for the Rothvale Gallery and shut off the engine. It was a dreary day, drizzling and chilly, but not inside my car. Having Brynne sitting next to me, dressed for work, looking beautiful, sexy, smiling at me, had me soaring, but knowing what we'd just shared together that morning was the fucking bomb. And I wasn't talking about the fucking. Remembering the shower and what we'd done there would hold me throughout my day—just barely, but it was knowing that I'd see her again tonight, that we'd be together, that she was mine, and that I could take her to bed and show her all over again. It was the conversation we'd had too. I felt like she'd finally let me in a little. That she cared about me in the same way I cared about her. And it was time to start talking future with us. I wanted so much with her.

"Did I ever tell you how much I like it when you smile at me, Ethan?"

"No," I answered, dropping the smile, "tell me."

She shook her head at my tactics and looked out the window at the rain. "I've always felt special when you do because I think you don't smile much in public. I would describe you as reserved. So when you smile at me I'm kind of . . . swept away."

"Look at me." I waited for her to respond, knowing it would come. This was another thing we had yet to discuss but was crystal clear from the very beginning. Brynne was naturally submissive to me. She accepted what I wanted to give her—the dom in me had found my muse, and it was just one more reason we were perfect together.

I sweep you away, huh?

She lifted her brown/green/gray eyes to me and waited while my cock pounded in my trousers. I could take her right here in the car and still want her minutes later. She was that much of an addiction.

"Christ, you're beautiful when you do that."

"Do what, Ethan?"

I tucked a strand of her silky hair behind her ear and smiled for her again. "Never mind. You just make me happy, is all. I love bringing you to your job after I've had you all night."

She blushed at me and I wanted to fuck her again.

No, that's not right. I wanted to make love to her— slowly. I could just picture her gorgeous body stretched out naked for me to pleasure in every way I could manage it. *All mine.* For me alone. Brynne made me feel everything—

"Would you like to come in and see what I'm working on? Do you have time?"

I brought her hand to my lips and breathed the scent of her skin. "I thought you'd never ask. Lead on, Professor Bennett."

She laughed. "Someday, maybe. I'll wear one of those black robes and glasses and do my hair up in a bun. I'll give lectures on proper conserving techniques, and you can sit in the back and distract me with inappropriate comments and leering."

"Ahhh, and will you summon me to your office for chastisement then? Will you detain me, Professor Bennett? I am sure we can negotiate a deal for me *working off* my disrespectful behavior." I put my head down toward her lap.

"You are insane," she told me, giggling and pushing me back. "Let's go inside."

We ran through the rain together, my umbrella shielding us, her slim shape tucked against me, smelling of flowers and sunshine and making me feel like the luckiest man on the planet.

She introduced me to the old security guard, who was clearly in love with her, and led me back into a great, studiolike room. Wide tables and easels were set up with good lighting and plenty of open space. She brought me up to a large oil painting of a dark-haired, solemn woman with startling blue eyes, holding a book.

"Ethan, please say hello to Lady Percival. Lady Percival, my boyfriend, Ethan Blackstone." She smiled at the painting like they were best friends.

I offered a half bow to the painting and said, "My lady."

"Isn't she amazing?" Brynne asked.

I studied the image pragmatically. "Well, she is an arresting figure, to be sure. She looks like she has a story behind her blue eyes." I peered closer to look at the book she held with the front visible. The words were hard to read, but once I realized they were French it was somewhat easier.

"I've been working on the section with the book in particular," Brynne said. "She suffered some heat damage in a fire decades ago and it's been a struggle getting the cooked-on lacquer off that book. It's special, I just know it."

I looked again and made out the word *Chrétien*. "It's in French. That is the name Christian right there." I pointed.

Her eyes got big and her voice excited. "It is?"

"Yes. And I'm sure this says *Le Conte du Graal*. The Story of the Grail?" I looked at Brynne and shrugged. "The woman in the painting is called Lady Percival, right? Isn't Percival the knight who found the Holy Grail in the King Arthur legend?"

"Good God, Ethan!" She grabbed my arm in excitement. "Of course! Percival . . . it's her story. You figured it out! Lady Percival is holding a very rare book indeed. I *knew* it was something special! One of the first King Arthur stories ever written down; all the way back in the twelfth century. That book is Chrétien de Troyes's *The Story of Perceval and the Grail*." She gazed at the painting, her face glowing with happiness and pure joy, and I reached for my mobile and snapped a picture of her. A magnificent profile shot of Brynne smiling at her Lady Percival.

"Well, I'm glad I could help you, baby."

She leapt at me and kissed me on the lips, her arms wrapped tightly around me. It was the most amazing feeling in the world.

"You did! You helped me so much. I'm going to call the Mallerton Society today and tell them what you discovered. They will be interested, I'm sure. There's his birthday exhibit coming next month . . . I wonder if they'll want to include this . . ."

Brynne rambled, excitedly telling me everything I could ever have wanted to know about rare books, paintings of rare books, and the conserving of paintings of rare books. Her face flushed with the thrill of solving a mystery, but that smile and kiss were worth their weight in gold to me.

I opened my eyes and tried to get my bearings. My head felt like I'd been smashed with a board. A half-empty bottle of Van Gogh stared at me. Djarum butts were sprinkled atop my desk where my cheek was stuck fast, filling my nose with the smell of stale cloves and tobacco. I peeled my face off the desktop and propped my head in my hands, supported on firmly planted elbows.

The same desk where I'd laid her out and fucked her only a few hours before. Yes, fucked. That had been pure, unapologetic shagging, and so good my eyes stung at the remembrance. The light on my mobile blinked madly. I flipped it over so I didn't have to look. I knew none of the calls were from her anyway.

Brynne wouldn't call me. Of that I was certain. The only question was how long before I tried calling her.

It was nighttime now. Dark outside. Where was she? Was she horribly hurt and upset? Crying? Being comforted by her friends? Hating me? Yeah, probably all of those, and I couldn't go to her and make it better either. *She doesn't want you.*

So this is what it feels like. Being in love. It was time to face some truths about Brynne and what I'd done to her. So I stayed in my office and faced it. I couldn't go home. There was too much of her there already, and seeing her things would only drive me utterly mad. I'd stay here tonight and sleep on sheets that didn't have her scent all over them. *Didn't have her in them.* A wave of panic sliced into me and I had to move.

I heaved my arse off the chair and stood up. I saw the scrap of pink fabric on the floor at my feet and knew what it was. The lacy knickers I'd peeled off her during that session on my desk.

Fuck! Remembering where I was when that message from her dad came through. *Buried inside her.* It was agonizing to touch something that had last been against her skin. I fingered the fabric and put them in my pocket. A shower was calling my name.

I went through the back door to the attached suite set up with a bed, a bath, a TV and a small kitchen—everything top of the line. The perfect bachelor crash pad for the busy professional man who works so late there's no point in driving home.

Or more like a fuck pad. This is where I brought women if I wanted to fuck them. Always after hours, of course, and they never stayed the whole night. I got my "dates" the hell out long before dawn. All of this was before I found Brynne. I never wanted to bring her here. She was different from the beginning. Special. *My beautiful American girl.*

Brynne didn't even know about this suite. She would have figured it out in two seconds flat and hated me for bringing her into it. I rubbed my chest and tried to still the ache that burned. I turned on the shower and got undressed.

As the hot water poured over me, I leaned against the tile and faced exactly where I was. *You're not with her! You made a cock-up of everything, and she doesn't want you now.*

My Brynne had left me for the second time. The first time she did it in stealth in the middle of the night because she was terrorized by a bad dream. This time she just turned and walked away from me without looking back. I could see it in her face, and it wasn't fear that made her leave. It was utter devastation at the betrayal, to find I had kept the truth from her. I had broken her trust. I'd wagered too high and lost.

The urge to pull her back and make her stay was so great I punched the wall and likely fractured something to keep from grabbing her. She told me never to contact her again.

I turned off the shower and stepped out, the desolate sounds of dripping water draining away, making my chest hurt worse from the hollowness. I pulled down a plush towel and shoved my head in it. I stared at my image in the mirror as my face was revealed. Naked, wet, and miserable. Alone. I realized another truth as I stared at my motherfucker arsehole self.

Never is a very long time. I might be able to give her a day or two, but *never* was irrefutably out of the question.

The fact that she still needed protection from a threat which could prove dangerous hadn't changed either. I couldn't allow anything to happen to the woman I love. *Never*.

I smiled into the mirror, my cleverness amusing even me in my sorry state, for I had just found a perfect example of the proper usage for the word *never*.